The Birthday Present
& Other Stories

Margaret Faulkner

Just Print IT! Publications
HUNTINGDON – ENGLAND

Other Books By Margaret Faulkner

A Village Childhood
Telling Tales

Published & printed in Great Britain by
Just Print IT! Publications
59 The Whaddons, Huntingdon, Cambs. PE18 7NW
Tel: 01480 450880
www.just-printit.com

The moral right of the author has been asserted
A CIP catalogue record of this book is available from the
British Library

Copyright © Margaret Faulkner 2008

JPIV2041108a

ISBN 978-1-902869-34-6

First Edition

All rights reserved; no part of this publication may be reproduced or transmitted by any means, electronic, mechanical, photocopying or otherwise, without the prior permission of the publisher.

DEDICATIONS

For my nieces Louise, Amanda, Joanne and Sarah, my great nieces Molly, Emma, Katie and Annabelle & my great nephews Curtis and Alexander.

ACKNOWLEDGMENTS

I would like to thank the following people for all their help and encouragement. My friend and neighbour Josie Green for her help with proof reading. My great nieces Molly and Emma for allowing me to include their poems in this book. My sisters Marion Corley and Irene Holohan for promoting and selling my books at every opportunity! My good friend Trevor Dean for being my computer guru, and his wife Mary for being the best friend anyone could wish for.

I would also like to thank everyone who bought my last two books, and who then took the trouble to make encouraging remarks about them. I hope they like this one too, even though it is very different from A Village Childhood and Telling Tales.

Thanks go also to all the Huntingdon Writers' Group members, for their encouragement, friendship and valuable feedback.

Lastly, thanks to Joanne and Jacky from Just Print It, for publishing books that I am proud of.

As always Cancer Research will benefit from the sales of all my books

Margaret Faulkner
November 2008

CONTENTS

5.	The Birthday Present	93.	May
16.	Green Fingers	95.	Stand And Deliver
17.	A Family Christmas	106.	Wood Smoke
22.	The Joys of Middle Age	109.	The Sunlit Morning
24.	Animals	110.	March
25.	Affair at Neptune's Beach	111.	Bewitched
33.	A Letter of Compliant	115.	The Leopard
35.	A Perfect Wedding	116.	The New Tenant
38.	Leopards and Spots	123.	My Mum
51.	First Day Back 1	124.	Encounter
55.	First Day Back 2	128.	The Proposal
59.	Bouquet	132.	Molly's Christmas Poem
61.	A Sanguine Affair	133.	Summons
63.	My People Next Door	134.	The Loving Niece
69.	New Year Ultimatum	138.	November
73.	Visions of Pompeii	140.	Timmy
74.	Eccentric Limerick	150.	Writing Exercise
75.	Skeleton In the Cupboard	152.	A Thank You Letter
77.	Poor Little Cow	154.	My Cousin Alex
88.	Love Story	155.	Happy Ever After
90.	Fred	160.	Angels
91.	April The Fool		

THE BIRTHDAY PRESENT

As Joy drove along in her ancient car, she smiled happily remembering the birthday cards she had received from her family and friends that morning.

The most striking one had been from her old school friend Anthea. Scrawled across the inside of the very expensive looking card were the words

"Happy birthday, darling! See you on our big day. Love from Anthea"

The thick purple writing was as flamboyant as the writer.

Joy and Anthea had been friends since they started school on their fifth birthday, fifty years ago today. Their shared birthday was the only thing that they really had in common. Anthea was an ambitious extrovert, whereas Joy was much quieter and had simpler tastes. It was the attraction of opposites that held their unlikely friendship together for many years.

When they left school Joy went into nursing, something she had always wanted to do. She worked hard and found great satisfaction in her vocation.

Anthea, a born organiser, soon turned her secretarial skills into her greatest asset. She changed companies regularly, always improving her status as she went. Before long she was personal assistant to the head of a large company. Eventually she married him, after he had divorced his wife.

Joy and Anthea met up occasionally before they married. They would have lunch, or perhaps a night at the theatre, but socially they were poles apart

After each had married, their meetings became fewer and fewer, until they no longer kept in touch at all.

Joy and John were happy for a few years, enjoying their comparatively simple life together, until John died suddenly of a heart attack, leaving Joy to bring up their two young children alone. She was devastated, but kept going for the sake of her son and daughter.

A couple of weeks ago Joy had come out of the supermarket in the little town where she had always lived, and literally bumped into Anthea.

They were both surprised and delighted to see each other again after such a long time and went into a nearby cafe for a coffee and to catch up with their news.

When they were shown to a table and seated, Anthea ordered their coffee. Joy took the opportunity to look more closely at her friend, and couldn't help feeling a little envious. Anthea's blonde hair was beautifully styled and she was expertly, but discreetly made up. She was expensively dressed in a cream linen suit, silk blouse and high heels. Her heavy gold earrings and necklace, were obviously the real thing, and must have cost a small fortune.. Everything about her said class.

Joy looked down at her own jeans and cheap turquoise t-shirt and felt very down market indeed beside her exotic friend.

While they waited for their coffee to arrive, Anthea patted Joy's hand and beamed at her.

"What a wonderful coincidence to bump into you like this!" she gushed. "It must be thirty years since we last met."

"At least," agreed Joy. "You look fantastic, Anthea, at least ten years younger than you are!"

"Thank you, darling. It's sweet of you to say so. Mind you, the odd little nip and tuck has helped." She laughed a deep throaty laugh.

"Are you still living in Hampstead?" Joy asked.

"No, darling." she answered, looking more serious. "Charles wasn't too well after he retired, so we decided to move to the country. I thought it would be ideal for us to come back to this area to live."

"Whereabouts are you living?"

"A little village about ten miles from here. Sedgley."

"I know it well." said Joy. "A beautiful spot."

It was one of Joy's favourite places. She and John had often driven there to look round. They knew that neither they, nor any other locals, could afford the pretty limestone houses, but it didn't stop them day dreaming.

"We'd only been there a couple of months, when Charles died. That was just three months ago. It was cancer."

"I am so sorry," Joy said sincerely. "How sad that he died so soon after moving here."

"A terrible blow. I know he was twenty five years older than me, but we were very close and had been together a long time. We hoped for a few more years." She sighed. "But it wasn't to be. I find it terribly lonely without him."

"I am sure that you do." agreed Joy. "I still miss John, and it's years since he died."

"So you are a widow too?" Anthea said sympathetically. "When did … ?"

"A long time ago. He was very young, it was a heart attack."

"Oh, you poor thing!" exclaimed Anthea. "How awful for you. Do you have any children?"

"Two. Paul is almost thirty and Judy is twenty-eight. They are both happily married and Judy has seven year old twin daughters. I love my grandchildren to bits. They give me so much pleasure. What about you?"

"I have one son." Anthea said proudly. "Piers. He is twenty seven and a great comfort to me now that I am alone."

"Does he live near you?"

"No, he has an art gallery in London, but he comes to see me when he can."

She looked at her watch.

"Good Heavens!" she exclaimed. "Is that really the time? Look, I really do have to go now. I have a hairdressers appointment. We must keep in touch now that we live almost next door to each other. We mustn't let another thirty years slip by, must we?"

She opened up her designer label leather handbag, fished around in it and pulled out a card and an expensive looking gold pen.

"Ah, here we are." she said handing Joy the card and pen. "Give me your number and I'll call you. I must fly now."

She planted a swift kiss on Joy's cheek and was gone in a whiff of expensive perfume.

༄༅

A few days later Anthea phoned as promised."Look, darling, I've been thinking," she said excitedly. "As it's our birthdays next week, we should have a little celebration. Come and have lunch with me on the big day and we can enjoy a leisurely meal and catch up on everything that has gone on during the last thirty years." she laughed her throaty laugh. "Don't you think that sounds like fun?"

"It sounds wonderful." agreed Joy. "Thank you, Anthea, I'd love to come."

On the day, Joy dressed carefully in her best navy and white two piece and crisp white blouse. She didn't think she looked too bad for fifty-five, but knew that Anthea would look even better.

It took her just under forty five minutes to reach Sedgley, and had no difficulty in finding Sunnybrook Cottage.

"Some cottage," she thought with a grin. It was the largest house in the village and had a large sloping lawn and colourful herbaceous borders.

Joy parked in the drive in front of the house, got out of the car and made her way to the front door. It opened before she had time to knock and Anthea, looking cool and elegant in apricot silk, came out to greet her.

"Darling!" she cried, wrapping her arms round her friend. "I have so been looking forward to seeing you again. Come on in."

She linked arms with Joy and led her through a large hallway into a long elegant drawing room. It was beautifully furnished with antiques. Two long low sofas were placed either side of a large open fireplace, which, since it was summer, had a tasteful flower arrangement in it. Nothing in the room clashed, or looked out of place. The restoration of the old cottage had been done with sympathy and excellent taste. The furnishings, the pictures, the gleaming wood of tables and chairs, must have cost a fortune, thought Joy, but it was worth it. Everything was just right.

"Happy birthday, Anthea." Joy said, handing her friend the bunch of lilies she had brought for her.

"Thank you, darling." gushed Anthea. "How clever of you to remember how much I loved lilies. I'll get Mrs. Bates to put them in water,"

She picked up a little package from the table.

"Hope you like this," she said with a smile. "Happy birthday to you too."

Anthea quickly ripped off the paper and gasped when she saw a little bottle of the very expensive Joy perfume.

"Anthea!" she exclaimed. "No one has ever bought me expensive perfume like this. It's wonderful! Thank you so much."

"My pleasure, darling," Anthea smiled. "I'm glad you like it. I thought it was appropriate. Now what would you like to drink? I've a rather good sherry, or would you prefer a G & T?"

"A gin and tonic would be perfect." said Joy, settling back into a comfortable easy chair. "I love this room, Anthea."

"Pretty, isn't it?" Anthea agreed as she poured the drinks, and handed Joy a delicate cut crystal glass and popped a slice of lemon into it.

She sat down next to her friend, and touched her glass against her's.

"Here's to us." she said. "Let's hope we see a lot more of each other in future."

"I'll drink to that," Joy smiled.

Anthea leaned back in her chair as she sipped her drink.

"Mrs. Bates, my treasure, is making lunch for us." she said. "I really don't know what I'd do without her. It's such a problem getting reliable staff, don't you find?"

Joy laughed and shook her head.

"Oh Anthea!" she said. "The only staff I have ever had to worry about was the Staff Nurse when I was a probationer!"

"Then you are very lucky, darling." continued Anthea. "When we lived in Hampstead it was a nightmare, But let's not talk about such boring things. Do tell me what you have been up to for the last 30 years."

"Well, when John died I was in deep shock, but I had the kids to think about, so couldn't spend a lot of time feeling sorry for myself. It wasn't easy, money was short, but they were great kids, who have turned into wonderful adults. Both are happily married, so I have a lot to be thankful for."

"I know you said Judy has twin daughters. Does Paul have children?"

"No," Joy looked sad for a moment. "They are having problems in that area, but hopefully they will solve them soon."

"Any men, darling?" Anthea asked with a sly smile.

"One or two over the years, but nothing serious," Joy blushed a little. "Except Jack, whose been around for a long time now."

"Aha!" laughed Anthea. "I thought as much! You are far too attractive to have stayed celibate."

"Actually, Jack has asked me to marry him," Joy shyly. "I think I may well accept."

"How exciting!" breathed Anthea. "Congratulations."

A plump, red-faced woman put her head round the door.

"Lunch is served, Mrs. D'Arcy." she said.

"Thank you, Mrs. Bates, we'll come through right away."

Anthea led her friend through to the dining room, which was furnished in the same elegant style as the rest of the house.

The large oval table was set with linen place mats and napkins. Cut glass sparkled and silver gleamed. A simple flower arrangement stood in the centre of the table.

Mrs. Bates served them with perfectly cooked salmon fillets in a cream and dill sauce. She placed a bowl of buttered new potatoes and a mixed salad on the table.

"Thank you, Mrs. Bates," Anthea said. "We will serve ourselves. It all looks delicious."

"Thank you, ma'am." Mrs. Bates said quietly and left.

Anthea reached for a bottle of champagne that had been resting in an ice bucket by the side of her chair.

"I thought we should have something a little special." she smiled. "Charles kept an excellent cellar and I adore champagne, don't you?"

"When I get the chance," laughed Joy. "But only a small one for me. I am driving you know."

Anthea expertly opened the bottle and poured the wine into cut glass flutes.

"Happy birthday again!" she said, touching her glass against Joy's.

Joy took a little sip and smiled.

"I am being thoroughly spoiled, Anthea. This meal really is wonderful. Thank you so much."

"Well, it isn't every day that one can celebrate a fifty-fifth birthday with a school friend. I am so glad that we bumped into each other last week."

"Me too." agreed Joy.

Mrs. Bates cleared away the first course and brought in a bowl of fresh raspberries and strawberries, with a large jug of cream.

"Mr. Bates is my gardener and he picked these berries this morning."

"They don't come a lot fresher than that," smiled Joy.

When they had finished Joy lay down her spoon and smiled contentedly.

"That was a perfect meal, Anthea. Absolutely delicious. Thank you again."

"My pleasure, darling," Anthea smiled. "Mrs. Bates will serve us coffee on the terrace. It'd such a lovely day we might as well sit in the garden."

When they were settled and sipping their coffee, Joy scanned the garden with envy. It was beautifully laid out and was well looked after.

"This really is a beautiful house." she said. "I do envy you living here."

"It is nice, isn't it?" agreed Anthea. "Charles loved it. We had hoped to spend many happy years here, but…" her voice trailed away.

"What a terrible shame." Joy sympathised. "Now," she added brightly. "Tell me about this son of yours."

"Piers is a great comfort to me. He's terribly clever. He has inherited his father's business acumen, and has this artistic flair as well."

She sipped her coffee and continued. "The gallery in London is doing very well. He specialises in contemporary artists and has this marvellous eye for talent.

His flat in Mayfair is a wonderful place, very modern and minimalist. It is such a delight to visit him there. There are always up and coming artists around the place. Such stimulating company."

"Is he married?" asked Joy.

Anthea looked away with a little shrug of her shoulders.

"No, darling, he isn't really the marrying kind."

"What a shame." exclaimed Joy. "Wouldn't you like grand-children?"

"Heavens no!" laughed Anthea. "I can't really see me as a grand-mother, can you?"

"Why ever not" Joy smiled serenely. "I adore the twins."

"I simply can't envisage Piers letting children run wild in his flat!" Anthea said with a wry smile. "And can you imagine kids in this house?"

"Maybe not." Joy smiled. "Is Piers coming to see you today?" she asked.

"I wish he could, but he is awfully busy. He did manage to spend a couple of days with me after Charles's funeral, but he can't neglect the gallery." She smiled quickly. "He did phone me this morning to wish me a happy birthday, so that was nice. He's a very thoughtful boy."

"You must miss him."

"Of course I do, darling, but he has his own life to lead. He has never really been around me a lot. He went to prep school, then boarding school and university, and after he graduated he spent a lot of time in San Francisco. When he came home he started the gallery, so he hasn't really lived at home for years."

"I'm lucky, I suppose." said Joy. "All my family live close by, so I see them frequently."

"Piers is very good to me, Joy." Anthea said quietly. "He's very generous." She stood up. "Come and see what he gave me for my birthday. I have been dying to show you."

She led Joy into a room at the back of the house. One wall was lined with books and a fine antique desk stood by the window. Anthea waved a slim hand round the room.

"This is my library and study." She grinned, "Which is a rather grand name for such a cosy room. I feel warm and safe here."

Joy looked round and could see why Anthea loved the room, it was as elegant as all the others, but the soft peach coloured décor gave it a cosy and welcoming atmosphere.

"I spend a lot of time in here. It's where I write my letters and read." She smiled broadly. "And that is why I wanted Piers present to be on the wall there."

She pointed to a picture that hung on the wall opposite the desk. It was a portrait of a handsome young man, with thick blonde hair, a sensuous mouth and sleepy blue eyes. His open necked shirt contrasted dramatically with his smooth tanned skin. The pose was indolent and sensual. It was a striking and vibrant picture.

"What an extraordinary painting." exclaimed Joy. "Is it an original?"

"Of course." smiled Anthea. "It is a Rudi Annello."

"I'm sorry, Anthea, but I'm afraid I am a complete philistine. Is he famous?"

"Almost," laughed Anthea. "He will be one day. Piers assures me that the picture will appreciate in value. Not that I am concerned about that. Rudi is a charming man, and extremely talented as you can see."

"Oh, so you actually know the artist, do you?" asked Joy. "How exciting! Did you meet him at the gallery?"

"He has a studio in Piers flat. They live together and have done for some time. They are very fond of each other."

"Oh, I see," Joy said quietly. "Do you know the model too?"

"It's Piers!" laughed Anthea. "I thought you realised."

"Of course, I can see the family likeness now." exclaimed Joy. "How silly of me not to realise. He's a wonderful looking young man. Did he commission it especially for you?"

"Yes." Anthea said proudly. "He wanted me to have something unique and help Rudi as well." She smiled warmly. "Rudi is a sweet boy, darling. Piers thinks very highly of his talent, and he's rather gorgeous as well."

"It is a beautiful painting. You must be delighted with such a wonderful birthday present."

"Oh I am, darling," agreed her friend. "Absolutely thrilled."

Anthea showed Joy round the rest of the house. Each room was perfect and expensively furnished in a style that suited the house and it's elegant occupant. Joy felt as if she were walking through a three dimensional illustration for an Ideal Home magazine.

At four o clock Mrs. Bates served them Earl Grey tea, tiny cucumber sandwiches and little home made cakes on the terrace.

When they finished tea, Joy looked at her watch.

"I really should go." she said. "The family are taking me out to dinner tonight. We are eating early because of the twins. Jack will be there too, so it should be fun."

"How lovely," said Anthea. "Are you going to the White Geranium?"

"No!" Laughed Joy. "That is far too grand for us. We usually go to the Fox. They do a great steak and chips there. It's not too expensive and very child friendly."

She put an arm around her friend.

"Thank you so much, Anthea, it's been wonderful. A perfect birthday treat."

"It's been lovely to see you again." Anthea kissed her friend's cheek. "We must do it again very soon."

As she drove home Joy thought about the visit, Anthea's obvious wealth, and the lovely things that surrounded her. She couldn't help a feeling of discontent niggling at her.

"What a wonderful place to live in," she thought. "All those perfect rooms, beautiful furniture, with everything co-ordinated." She sighed. "My poor old furniture has seen better days. The carpet is wearing thin and the dining table has that horrible mark where Paul stood his hot coffee cup."

The feeling of envy grew. "The curtains are faded and nothing matches. It's a complete mess!" She shook her head sadly. "Then there's Anthea herself. Well preserved, slender, perfectly made-up and expensively dressed. That pale apricot suit was the perfect colour and style for her. I felt decidedly dowdy in my best navy and white!"

She smiled grimly.

"And that picture! Not a massed produced print, but an exquisite portrait of her son painted by a soon-to-be famous artist whose a family friend. Who could top that?"

When she entered her house she looked round in despair. Everything looked shabby and lack-lustre after the wonderful things she had seen in Sunnybrook Cottage.

Anthea had given her a lovely day, but had also made her feel discontented with her lot.

ೀಚ

Later, as Joy and her family gathered round the large table at the Fox, she cheered up.

The food was good, attractively served and the portions generous.

"OK," She thought. "So it's not fine dining at the White Geranium, but at least my lovely family are paying a price that they can afford."

"Are you OK, Mum?" asked Judy, placing a hand over Joy's. "You seem a bit quiet tonight."

"I'm fine," Joy smiled. "I am just recovering from a bit of Anthea-itus!"

She told them of her day and described the wonders of Sunnybrook Cottage and her friend Anthea D'Arcy.

"She is a very rich and lucky woman." she declared when she finished.

"It all sounds wonderful." Judy said softly.

When the meal was over Joy noticed an air of excitement about the family. Elena and Emma were bright-eyed and giggling together and could hardly keep still.

A waitress brought out a large iced cake, inscribed with her name and ablaze with candles. It was placed before her and everyone sang Happy Birthday to her when she blew out the candles.

The cake was cut and a bottle of sparkling wine was opened and shared amongst the adults.

"Not quite like the vintage champagne I shared with Anthea at lunchtime." she thought, then immediately felt mean for even thinking it.

When they were sipping their wine, Paul cleared his throat.

"Mum, Kay and I have something to tell you." He smiled at his radiant young wife. "We are going to have a baby."

Joy leapt up and hugged them both.

"That is great news" she cried with tears in her eyes. "I am so happy for you."

When everyone had congratulated the young couple, Jack stood up.

"Time for your presents now. Come on, everyone, bring out your parcels."

"The family has clubbed together to buy you something." said Judy. "We hope you like it."

She tore open the packet and found a little box, inside which was a gold locket on a slender chain.

"It's beautiful," she said. "Thank you so much."

But she hated herself for thinking that it wasn't quite as heavy and expensive as Anthea's gold necklace.

Jack took her hand and before she realised it, he had slipped a ring onto the third finger of her left hand. She looked down at it and her heart skipped a beat when she saw the pretty Victorian opal and seed pearl ring that she knew had once been his mother's.

"You know what I am asking, don't you?" He said gently. "Will you?"

Blushing like a school girl, Joy nodded.

"Yes Jack, of course I will."

Everyone cheered and congratulated them and another bottle of wine was ordered.

Emma came and stood by her grandmother.

"Granny, Elena and me have got a present for you too."

Elena joined her twin and stood the other side of Joy.

Each placed an envelope on the table.

"I'm three minutes older that Emma," said Elena "So open mine first."

Joy picked up the envelope and opened it and drew out a childish picture of a woman with a big smiley face.

"I drew it for you, Granny, it's a picture of you." A slight frown crossed her face. "I tried really hard, but I couldn't get it to look as pretty as you though."

A lump rose in Joy's throat, but before she could speak Emma urged her to open her envelope.

"Mine's a picture of your house," Emma said, with a smile. "It's the best house in the world, 'cos you're inside it. We love you lots, don't we, Elena?"

"Yes, lots and lots" Agreed her twin.

The two little girls hugged their grandmother and Joy buried her head against their soft curls, as tears filled her eyes.

When her granddaughters had returned to their chairs, Joy looked at the childish daubs and her heart filled with love for her family and again her eyes brimmed with tears of happiness.

"They are the most beautiful pictures I have ever seen," she said truthfully. "And I am the happiest and luckiest woman in the world. Thank you everyone for making this the perfect birthday. I love you all so much."

ಸಂಞ

That night in bed Joy thought of Anthea, alone in her beautiful house, with only an oil painting of her son to keep her company and she felt a deep pang of pity for her friend..

"You may be wealthy, Anthea," she said aloud, "But I am the rich one."

Green Fingers

I've been working away in my garden
I've dug it and weeded and hoed
I've sprayed all the bugs and the green fly
I've mulched and I've planted and sowed.

I put well-rotted compost upon it
I've pruned and I've trimmed and I've raked
The stepped back to admire all its glory
It was worth it, although my back ached.

Then a friend came by just to see it
"You must have green fingers." she said,
"Not so much green." was my answer,
"Just blistered and sore, rough and red!"

A FAMILY CHRISTMAS

Millie picked up the envelope from the door mat. The Christmas card was from a couple she and Len had met on holiday five or six years ago. They always sent a card. Millie tried to remember if she had sent them one. Probably not. Writing the cards had always been Len's job.

Len had loved Christmas. She too had enjoyed all the planning and shopping for the extra special goodies she needed to make her puddings and cake. Len liked to stir the rich, spicy pudding mixture. He always followed tradition and made a wish. They enjoyed the little sample that she made for them to try. He never failed to say the same thing every time.

"Better than ever, love."

There had been no pudding ritual this year. What was the point? This would be the third Christmas without Len, but the first time she would be spending the festive season entirely alone.

Last year, Brian, her youngest son and his wife had invited her to spend Christmas Day with them. They had collected her in the morning and brought her home after tea. It had been nice, although it didn't feel the same as the days when they all came home for Christmas.

What days they had been! The house full of laughter, the smell of roasting turkey (which was always the largest the butcher could supply!). How she had loved to hear the excited shrieks of the children as Len, clad in a red dressing gown, ho, ho, ho-ed pretending to be Santa Claus, as he handed out the gifts.

She thought about the big dining room table groaning with every kind of seasonal fare, with balloons, crackers and paper hats.

She remembered the way her three handsome sons, their pretty wives and adorable children had gathered round them in a warm circle of love. She and Len were never happier than when surrounded by their adored family.

Millie sighed. Now they were all scattered around the world.

Four years ago their eldest son Michael, his beautiful American wife Nancy and two children had moved to New York to live. The same year their middle son, John, and his family had emigrated to Australia.

Soon after their departure Len started to have health problems, then three years ago he suffered a massive heart attack and died soon after in hospital. Millie was by his side and wished she could have died too.

She dreaded the first Christmas without Len, but come November she made her batch of puddings as usual, baked a cake and made plans for the usual family Christmas she knew would never happen.

Brian and his family joined her for Christmas lunch, but by mid-afternoon they had left. The magic had gone.

This year Brian had taken his family to New York to spend Christmas with Michael. Brian was a good boy and had asked her to join them. He even offered to pay her fare, but she smiled her thanks and shook her head.

"Thank you, love," she said, giving him a hug. "It's kind of you to offer, but I wouldn't want to be away from home at this time of year."

"Are you sure you will be all right, Mum?" Brian asked anxiously. "I hate to think of you being on your own."

"I'll be fine, love." Millie said. "I will enjoy the peace and quiet. I'm too old for all the fuss and bother of Christmas nowadays."

She almost believed it.

On the morning of Christmas Eve Millie looked round her sparsely decorated lounge and shook her head. She'd only put up a few strands of tinsel, some holly round the pictures and her Christmas cards.

"Not like the old days, eh, Len?" she said aloud.

She often talked to him. It was a hard habit to break after forty five happy years together.

"Sorry there's no tree, love." she continued apologetically. "There didn't seem much point, since there's only me to see it."

It was getting light, so she drew back the curtains.

A movement in the garden caught her eye.

"There's that scruffy cat again!" she said crossly. "Must be that a stray."

She opened the window.

"Shoo!" she yelled. "Clear off!"

The bedraggled cat slunk away behind her garden shed.

"It's probably one of those feral cats like I saw in that TV show." she muttered. "Just wild things, not at all like the fat sleek pets around here."

This one looked quite well fed though, in spite of its scruffy appearance. It probably raids dustbins, she thought with a shudder.

"Whatever it is, I am not having a filthy animal taking up residence in my shed. He has to go."

She put on her coat.

"Time I went into town to get my shopping, it is bound to be busy." she thought. "I will deal with the cat when I get home, if he is still here."

A chill sleety drizzle was falling when she got off the bus, so she hurried to the supermarket and joined the throng of housewives pushing their laden trolleys round the store, as they tried to control their over-excited offspring.

Millie picked up a basket and had soon completed her purchases.

She looked sadly at the contents of her basket as she queued at the check out. A tiny Christmas pudding in a tin foil basin, lay beside a packet of frozen chicken joints, some Brussels sprouts in a plastic bag, along with a few carrots. A small loaf, a mini packet of mince pies and a tub of cream and some frozen roast potatoes..

She felt tears stinging her eyes when she thought of all the wonderful Christmas dinners she had cooked for her family. What a pale imitation of festive fare she had bought today.

Back at home, as she put away her purchases, the tears that had been threatening all day coursed unchecked down her cheeks.

Quickly she dashed them away with her fist.

"Silly old fool!" she scolded herself. "What's the point in all this self pity? You could have been in New York if you hadn't been so stubborn!"

She busied herself by making a cup of coffee, spiced with a nip of brandy from the medicine cupboard.

She drank it as she sat by the fire and soon the warmth began to spread through her and she felt a little better.

As she rinsed her cup, she looked out of the window and saw the cat again. It looked startled and quickly disappeared, squeezing itself under the shed door.

"Oh no!" Millie said firmly. "You are not taking up residence in my shed. I don't want cat-mess everywhere."

She strode over to the shed and opened the door.

"Out you come! You can't stay in there."

She peered into the dim interior, but couldn't see the cat.

Seeing a slight movement under a pile of potato sacks, she got a hoe and began prodding at them.

A furious ball of bedraggled fur flew from the sacking, arching its back and spitting at her, green eyes blazing with anger.

Millie drew back, surprised at the cat's fury. She had expected it to run off, but it stood its ground, showing its teeth, its back arched and ears flattened to its head, prepared to attack if she came any closer.

Then Millie saw a movement from the sacking and heard a soft mewing noise. When her eyes had become accustomed to the gloom, she eased back the sacking with the hoe and saw a squirming bundle of black and white fur. The cat had a litter of kittens.

Millie's face softened and she put down the hoe.

"All right, puss." she cooed. "I see what you have there. Brave little mum, protecting her family. Come on, I won't hurt your babies."

Millie made soft noises and held out her hand, and eventually the cat relaxed, sensing that her babies weren't in any danger from this person. She lay down beside the kittens and began to lick them and they immediately began to suckle noisily.

"Well!" exclaimed Millie. "No wonder you looked well fed! You are looking a whole lot skinnier now, that's for sure." She looked round the shed and shook her head.

"It's turning a lot colder now, so I can't leave you here. You'll have to come up into the house."

Before long Millie had the little family ensconced in a cardboard box by the kitchen fire, wrapped in Len's old red dressing gown.

"There you are, puss." she said. "Your babies are warm and safe now, so I think it is time we got some food into you. You are such a skinny little thing, aren't you?"

She opened a tin of sardines, put them into a dish and fed them to the cat. Although she was obviously very hungry, the cat ate delicately as she crouched over the food, her pink tongue lapping quickly at the fish. When she had eaten her fill, she groomed herself, lying in front of the fire, stretching and purring, whilst her kittens snuffled and mewed in their box.

Millie picked up one of the tiny sightless kittens, She held it to her cheek and marvelled at the soft downy fur. A great tenderness swept over her when she realised how helpless it was. She placed it back beside its mother, who snuggled it against her body and began to lick it gently.

"I shall call you, Holly" Millie told the cat. "I think the name suit's a Christmas cat, don't you?"

It was late when Millie went to bed. She found it hard to drag herself away from Holly and her babies.

Christmas Day dawned cold and bright. As soon as Millie went into the kitchen Holly greeted her by rubbing round her legs.

"Happy Christmas to you and your babies," Millie said happily.

They shared the breakfast porridge that Millie made, Holly getting the top of the milk on hers. "You need building up," Millie said.

After washing the dishes and preparing their lunch, Millie sat by the fire. Holly jumped onto her lap, purring loudly as Millie stroked her soft fur. She looked down at the sleeping kittens and sighed happily.

"It's nice to have a family around us at Christmas, isn't it, Len?" she said softly. "Not quite like the old days, but I think Holly and her babies need me just as much as you and the boys did all those years ago," She sighed gently.

"Happy Christmas, Len."

Millie dozed by the cosy warmth of the fire. She may have been dreaming, but she was sure she heard Len's familiar voice reply.

"Happy Christmas, love."

The Joys Of Middle Age
(Written circa 1990)

I'm your average middle-aged woman.
And not particularly tough,
But I am sure the middle-aged movie star
Is made of much sterner stuff.

I bet that lovely Joan Collins
(Who is even older than me!)
Doesn't have one varicose vein
(At least not where one can see!)

Does Brigitte Bardot get hot flushes?
That make her drip with sweat
Spoiling her tousled hair style
By getting it soaking wet.

When Sophia Loren goes out dancing
Disco-ing all the night through
I bet that her feet don't hurt her
Or swell like mine always do.

The Joys Of Middle Age (Continued)

Does La Lollo have bi-focals?
Are her high heeled shoes double E?
Does rock music give her a headache?
Does she fall asleep watching TV?

I can't imagine Liz Taylor
In support hose boringly brown,
And I am sure she doesn't wear long-line bras
Beneath her clinging silk gown.

I suppose that there are compensations
For being the way that we are
It must be exhausting to constantly sparkle
Like the beautiful aging star!

A Poem for Aunty Margaret
(Written by Emma Holohan-Green in June 2008 aged 8)

ANIMALS

The baby rabbits hop-hopping in the morning light
The parents are chasing each other around.
They all cuddle together one, two three,
then here comes the dad ... whee!
We put them in a run and watch them all huddle up to each other.
A very nice sight to see.

AFFAIR AT NEPTUNE'S BEACH

Polly was glad when she saw the removal van at the house next door. It had been empty for too long.

Workmen had been there for sometime, making alterations and Polly had given them tea in exchange for information, and learned that her new neighbour was young and single, but handicapped, hence the major alterations to the building, which were needed to accommodate his wheel chair.

Now it looked as if he was moving in at last and Polly was curious to meet him. She realised that he must be reasonably well-off, because the house, even before its extensive make-over, was large and elegant, complete with a swimming pool.

When the vans were unloaded and the furniture put into the house, the removal men locked up and left, leaving Polly disappointed at not seeing the new owner.

The next morning Polly took her coffee and toast onto the patio, intending to make the most of what was going to be yet another perfect summer day. Glancing over the fence to next door she saw a young man in a wheel chair by the pool.

Spotting her he waved.

"Good morning!" he called.

"Hi!" she replied, shielding her eyes from the sun. "Lovely day, isn't it?"

She walked over to the fence. "Welcome to Neptune's Beach."

"Thank you."

As she drew nearer the fence and she could see her new neighbour more clearly, her heart skipped a beat. He was gorgeous!

His fashionably cut hair was blonde, his skin was tanned and the bright blue polo shirt he wore fitted tightly across his broad chest and muscular shoulders. A dark blue rug covered his legs.

"I'm Polly," she called.

"Look," he said, "It isn't easy talking at this distance, why don't you came and have a glass of orange juice with me, we can introduce ourselves properly, then you can tell me a little about the place."

"OK, that's great," Polly agreed. "Be with you in minute."

She dashed into her house and quickly ran a comb through her long dark hair, touched her full lips with a pale lip gloss and looked at herself in the mirror. Her smooth skin was sun tanned, so she didn't need any other make-up and within minutes she joined her new neighbour by his pool.

"Hi again!" he called as she approached, holding his hand out in greeting. "I'm Sandy Roxton. Delighted to meet you."

Polly was surprised at the coolness of his big brown hand when she shook it.

"I'm Polly Sealand and I am so happy to meet you at last." she laughed, "I have been wondering for ages who my new neighbour would be."

Sandy's sea-green eyes crinkled in a welcoming grin, and Polly thought she had never seen such a beautiful young man before and judging my his smooth tanned skin, she guessed that he spent a lot of time outdoors. "And by the looks of those muscles," she thought, "I'd say he worked out."

Sandy gestured to Polly to sit down and poured her a glass of orange juice from the jug that was set on a little wrought iron table by the pool.

"Have you lived in Neptune's Beach very long?" he asked, as he handed her the glass.

"About six years." she replied. "We moved here when we first got married."

She couldn't help noticing a little frown cross his face.

"Ah, you're married then?"

"Widowed," Polly corrected, "My husband was killed in a car crash last year."

"I am so sorry." Sandy said sincerely. "How dreadful for you."

"Yes," she agreed with a sad little smile. "It was terrible time, but I am getting over it very slowly. Every day it's a little better."

"Good," Sandy said sympathetically. "Now you must tell me all about Neptune's Beach."

"There's not a lot to tell," she said with a laugh. "It's just a small town, with some pretty buildings, a beautiful beach, with some rocks and cliffs. There are some lovely scenic walks." She blushed and looked down at his rug-covered legs. "Oh, I am so sorry, I didn't mean …" Her words trailed off and she went bright red with embarrassment.

"Don't worry," Sandy said with a laugh. "I am pretty mobile in this chair of mine. Maybe you could show me some of these lovely walks?"

"Of course, I'd love to," she said, his gracious acceptance of her apology making her feel at ease again.

"I really love the sea," he continued. "It's why I chose to come here to live."

"Where are you from originally?" she asked.

"I spent my childhood in Cornwall, but we moved to London, to help me with my music career." He sighed. "My mother died recently, and that's why I decided I needed to make a complete change and come back to live by the sea."

"So we have both suffered a recent bereavement." Polly said sympathetically. "I am so sorry."

"We must cheer each other up." he grinned and added. "My mother adopted me when I was a baby. She devoted her life to me, which wasn't easy for her considering my ..." He glanced down at his immobile legs.

"Have you always ...?" Polly asked shyly.

"Yes, always," he nodded.

He smiled suddenly, almost dazzling her with his good looks.

"However, life is good." he said " I'm successful at what I do, so I was able to repay her for her years of devotion. Her last few years were very comfortable."

"What do you do?"

"I'm a singer song-writer, so you will probably hear me singing and playing at times." He laughed. "You must tell me if it annoys you."

"I'm sure it won't," Polly smiled. "I love music. Maybe you will let me hear some of your songs one day."

He leaned toward her and squeezed her hand gently, making her heart pound.

"Yes, I'd really like that." he said softly.

"Do you swim?" he asked, his manner suddenly becoming brisk and business-like.

"Yes," Polly nodded. "I try to swim everyday in the summer. I go to one of the quieter beaches, but they are so busy in the holiday season."

"Then you must use my pool whenever you want to."

"That is very kind of you," she smiled. "I may well take you up on that. Thank you very much.!"

"Good, I love to swim too," he took her hand again. "I think we are going to be very good neighbours." He picked up his glass. "Let's drink to that."

Polly clinked her glass against his, nodding her agreement.

She drained her glass and stood up.

"I have to go," she said. "I need to go to the shops. Can I get anything for you."

"No thanks, I brought plenty of goods with me, but do call again soon. And don't forget to use the pool whenever you want to."

Back in her own house Polly felt a surge of excitement. Not since Mark had been killed had she felt such an attraction to anyone. Sandy, she supposed, was about her own age, late twenties to early thirties, with a warm and friendly personality, plus film star good looks. She couldn't believe her good fortune at having someone so nice as a neighbour.

When she returned from the shops, she made a salad for her lunch, then slipped into her sleek black swimsuit. She knew it was flattering, because Mark always complimented her on how gorgeous she looked in it. She blushed a little thinking how much she wanted to make a good impression on Sandy. She wrapped a colourful sarong around her and made her way round to Sandy's house, taking with her the flowers she had bought in the village for him.

Polly tapped on the open kitchen door and entered. Sandy was sitting by the table, where the remains of his lunch was still on the table. He was gently strumming on a guitar.

He looked up and greeted her warmly.

"Hi!" he said softly. "So glad you came back."

"I have brought you some flowers as a house warming present," she said. "Shall I put them in water for you?"

"What a sweet gesture." He took the flowers and smelled them. "They are gorgeous. Yes, you will find a vase on that windowsill."

Polly filled the vase with water and arranged the white roses. She put the vase in the middle of the table, and automatically cleared away his plate and put them in the sink.

"Ah," he grinned. "The woman's touch."

"Sorry," she said, blushing again. "It's force of habit."

"It's what I've missed since Mum died." He said with a smile.

"I see you have come prepared to swim," he continued. "Good, it is so hot today it will do you good."

He wheeled his chair alongside her and they went through the French windows.

"Have fun," he said. "I'll see you later, I have work to do."

Polly was disappointed that he didn't stay, but quickly slipped off the sarong and dived into the cool blue waters of the pool. She was a strong swimmer and had soon completed several lengths. Eventually she pulled herself out and sat on the edge, drying her hair.

Sandy joined her and offered her a glass of lemonade.

"Thank you," she sighed happily. "That was great!"

"You are a very strong swimmer," he said, his voice full of admiration.

"Yes, and I've got medals to prove it." she laughed. "I have always felt at home in the water."

"Me, too."

"Why didn't you join me?" she asked. "It would have been fun."

"One day I will." he said softly.

And so it began, the friendship that was to change Polly's life completely.

As the hot summer continued the pattern of her days became centred around afternoons spent in Sandy's pool. She was disappointed that he never joined her in the water, although she did sometimes hear him splashing about late at night when she was in bed. The hauntingly strange and beautiful songs he sang filled her with strange feelings of longing that she didn't understand. They wove spells around her heart.

They would also go for walks along the cliff paths. He in his wheel chair and she walking alongside. They enjoyed the scenery and the ever changing colours of the sea. Polly hadn't been so happy since before she was widowed and Sandy seemed to feel the same.

About a month after their first meeting Sandy kissed her.

She was sitting by the pool, towelling her hair after a swim, when he reached out to touch her cheek. He bent down and their lips touched.

His mouth tasted cool and salty as she responded warmly. Through half closed eyes she saw his tanned face. Over-laid with a bluish tinge from the reflected water, giving him an unearthly masculine beauty.

He stroked back the damp hair from her face and kissed her again.

"Come and swim with me," she pleaded. "You never have and it could be such fun."

His eyes looked troubled and he tightened his grip on her.

"I'm afraid to," he whispered. "I couldn't bear to see you look at my misshapen body with disgust. I swim in the dark so no one can see me."

"But …" Polly started to protest, but Sandy gently put his finger against her mouth.

"Shh," he said softly. "not now, Polly. One day, but not now."

Eventually Polly stopped protesting and simply enjoyed the fact that he had wanted to kiss her.

༄༅

As the summer progressed, they made daily excursions to the beach or onto the cliffs. Polly would make a picnic and he would bring along his guitar. She would sit on a rug and serve the food, while he played his music and sang softly to her. They spent happy hours basking in the sunshine, the joy of each others company and their fast growing affection for each other.

Towards the end of August when they were sitting by the pool, Polly felt suddenly sad.

"Summer will soon be over and I'll miss my swim in your pool and these trips to the beach." she said. "I don't like the winter."

"I don't either and I'll miss all this too."

Sandy suddenly looked very serious. He took her hand and looked deeply into her eyes.

"I have something I must say to you."

"What is it?" Polly looked anxious.

"I have fallen in love with you. I know we have only known each other a short time, but I have never been so sure of anything before in my life." The coolness of his hands on hers startled her the way it always did. "Would you consider spending the rest of your life with me?"

"Oh, Sandy." Polly breathed. "Of course I will. I love you too."

He gripped her hand tightly.

"Of course, there are difficulties you must consider."

Polly laid a finger against his lips,

"Shh," she said. "nothing matters and we can overcome anything if we love each other."

"Please, Polly, let me finish. Yes, there are difficulties, but we can be happy together. However, it is you who will have to make all the sacrifices. Are you prepared for that?"

Polly looked deeply into his eyes.

"With you, Sandy, anything is possible." She kissed him. "Anything at all."

"Before you make up your mind, I have to tell you a little about myself.

I told you that I was adopted, didn't I? This is the whole story.

When my mother was a young woman she was walking on a beach in Cornwall and she found me lying in a rock pool. A tiny baby close to death.

Of course, she could see that I was handicapped, but she still took me home and cared for me. She didn't report her find to anyone, but decided to bring me up herself. Things were difficult for both of us, but she brought me up to be as independent as possible, preparing me for a future when she wasn't around anymore. to look after me. She encouraged me in my musical career and we even moved to London so that I had greater opportunities than I had in Cornwall. Thank goodness, my career was successful and I made enough money to keep her in comfort when she got sick. She had always guided me through life and she even told me that I was to look for a certain sort of girl to marry. She could have been describing you!"

Polly smiled. "I wish I had known her."

"She would have loved you." Sandy continued. "I have avoided showing you my disfigured body, but now is the time. Are you strong enough, Polly?"

"I love you, Sandy," Polly said as she placed her arms around him. "And that means everything about you.. Nothing about you could upset me."

That night Polly lay in Sandy's arms, happy and contented after their first swim in the pool together. The night air was warm and heavy with the scent of stocks and lilies, as they lazily swam together in the velvet darkness. They kissed and embraced, delighted in the mutual pleasure of being together.

As they lay in each other's arms, Sandy told her of his early life and his desire to return to his roots, taking Polly with him as his bride.

His words and the strange songs he sang wove around her brain and heart and she knew that she would go with him wherever he wanted to go and be with him forever.

The next day as they ate breakfast together, Sandy squeezed Polly's hand.

"The weather will break today, " he said. "So let's go to the cliff for the last time."

Polly prepared a picnic as usual, then she pushed the wheel chair to the top of the cliff, and made their way to the most secluded place they knew. The sun still shone warmly, but Polly shivered from time to time. She was happier than she had ever been, but knew her life was about to change forever. She couldn't help feeling a little nervous.

When they had eaten their picnic and cleared away the litter, Sandy called her to him.

"Come here to me, Polly."

She went and stood beside him.

He looked into her eyes.

"Are you really sure?"

"Absolutely," she said with conviction.

"Then we'll do it now." He smiled at her reassuringly. "Take off your dress."

She obeyed and stood naked before him.

"You are so beautiful, and you love me enough to do this. Are you completely sure."

"Yes, I've never been so sure of anything before."

"Then do it."

Polly pushed the wheel chair to the edge of the cliff. There was a sheer drop down to the sea, which sparkled like sapphires in the afternoon sun.

She stopped when she got as close to the edge as possible.

Sandy threw off the blanket that covered his lap. Then with great strength, he hauled himself out of his chair and launched himself over the edge of the cliff.

Polly watched in awe as his tanned body described an arc against the blue sky, before dropping into the water of the incoming tide. His broad shoulders and chest tapered down into slim hips that ended in a spectacular fish-tail that glittered, green, blue and purple in the sunlight. He entered the water with barely a splash, he surfaced then held up an arm.

"Come, Polly, we must go home."

Polly looked at the deserted wheel chair and the crumpled heap of her discarded dress, then hearing the strange and haunting song coming from Sandy's lips, she laughed aloud with joy and leapt from the cliff into his open arms.

They dived, and as the water closed over her head, Polly felt her heart leap with joy.

Sandy took her hand and led his bride down into his watery kingdom to fulfil his destiny.

༄༅

The locals still talk about the strange affair at Neptune's Beach and the disappearance of the pretty widow and the tragically handicapped young musician. Was it an accident? Maybe it was a suicide pact. Their bodies were never found, but on still warm summer evenings it is said that strange music can be heard drifting in on the tide.

A LETTER
OF COMPLAINT

The Writer's Group exercise was to write a letter of complaint. It could be fact or fiction. I wrote this as a sort of protest about Vanity Publishing and the adverts for would-be writers to sign up to write a book., no matter whether they had a talent for writing or not.

Ivor Little-Tallant
Book End Cottage
Grate Reeding
Aisle of White

The Manajing Dyrecter
Van Atee Publishing
Conham
Reading

Dere Sur,

Sum thyme ago I replyed to yaw advert in one of them Sundy papers, wear yew promised to publish novells for fokes if they payed yew a substashal fee of free farsand pahnds. I was good at English and spellin at skool, so fort I'd ave a go and send you one of the composishuns wot I rote.

Yew sed that on receet of me check yew wood print it up fer me, do all the adverts and sell a lot of me books and make me pots of munny. That made me very appy I can tell yer, coz I aint never writ nuffin like this befour and I was a bit surprised abaht it. Anyway, I dun wot yew wanted and sent off me storey and check strait away. It were a goodun, as yew no, wiv lotsa vilince and mucky bits. Me missis sed it was disgustin, so I no it were good. I bet you fort so too, Ope it didn't make yew blush.

Anyway that were free munfs ago and I aint erd nuffin from yer, aint ad no munny or books from yew. So wots goin on?

Yew sed in yaw ad that if me book didn't do no good yew wood refund me munny, so I sugest yew do that strate away. I can then send me manu.. Manew.. Manyewskript to annuvver publisher wot appreciates me storey and pays me the farsands of pahnds its worf.

If yew don't do this wivin the next week I will be in tuch wiv me breef, who will soon sort yew aht, or failin that I will be forced to send the boys rahnd … and yer no wot that means don't yew? Im shore I don't ave to spell it aht.

YEW AVE BIN WARND!

Yer obedient servent

Ivor Little Tallant
(Orfer)

A PERFECT WEDDING

Mark closed the door of the hotel room leaned against it and smiled at his wife.

"Thank goodness for that," he said with a deep sigh. "I thought we would never get away."

Kate sat on the edge of the bed, kicked off her high heeled shoes and rubbed her feet ruefully.

"We'd better not be too long," she said. "The disco will be starting soon."

"I know," Mark said wearily, taking off his tail coat and shaking out the confetti. "But we've got a few minutes, haven't we? I need a bit of a breather before we change."

He quickly stripped to his underwear and lay down on the bed.

"Me too," agreed Kate, then turning her back to him she said. "Unzip me please, darling."

Mark propped himself up on his elbow and slowly eased the long zip down Kate's slim back. She stood up and slid the lace dress over her shoulders and hips and stepped out of it.

Mark lay back on the bed, his hands clasped behind his head, watching his wife's striptease with interest.

"Very nice," he said appreciatively. "Very nice indeed! You know, you looked beautiful today, Kate. That dress is perfect. I am really proud of you."

"Thank you, darling," smiled Kate, throwing the discarded dress over the back of a chair and smiling happily at her husband. "It cost a fortune, but it was worth it, even if it is only for one day's wear."

She lay down beside him on the bed. The pale slinky expensive silk slip feeling sensuous and deliciously wicked against her skin. She shuddered with pleasure.

They lay still for a moment, close but not touching.

"It was a perfect wedding, wasn't it, Mark?"

"Absolutely wonderful," agreed Mark, then he chuckled. "Your mother cried!"

"So did yours," laughed Kate. "She pretended not to, but I saw her dabbing her eyes surreptitiously." She looked a little sheepish.

"I almost did!" she confessed.

"It's allowed, isn't it?"

"Not really, only the brides mother is supposed to weep!"

Mark shifted slightly on the bed and took Kate's hand in his.

"The caterers did a fantastic job. I really enjoyed the food." he said with relish. "And the champagne was wonderful!"

"Trust you to think of your stomach!" teased Kate "it was the church that brought a lump to my throat, It looked absolutely wonderful and weren't the flowers gorgeous."

She smiled dreamily. "The little bridesmaids looked adorable. In fact, they all looked pretty, didn't they?"

"Especially Tracey" Mark said with a leer.

Kate dug him in the ribs with her elbow.

"You were not supposed to notice Tracey."

"She's hard not to notice! All that bosom, blonde hair, lips and teeth!" He laughed. "You have to admit that her dress was rather low cut, wasn't it?"

"Maybe, but you shouldn't have noticed it today. It's not proper!"

"Is it all right to be IM-proper with you today?" Mark asked with a cheeky grin, then turning on his side he ran his hand over Kate's stockinged thigh and up under the lacy hem of her slip and gently snapped her suspender.

"I find these stockings very sexy, Mrs. Jones. You are a very lovely lady."

"Better than Tracey?" Kate asked, twining her arms round him and moving closer.

"Much, much better than Tracey." he whispered against her neck.

"Then you had better remember that, okay?" she murmured as she kissed him.

A loud knocking on the door startled them, and the familiar voice of Kate's mother brought them sharply down to earth.

"Come on, you two." she called. "Whatever are you doing? Are you nearly ready? The disco has already started. You're missing all the fun!"

"Wanna bet,?" Mark whispered in Kate's ear, as he held her tightly to him.

Kate giggled softly.

"We won't be long Mum." she called. "We're just getting changed."

"Well, hurry up. People are asking where you are."

They heard her walking away and they both heaved a sigh of relief.

"She's gone." whispered Mark. "Now where was I before I was so rudely interrupted?"

"Come on," Kate said, swinging her legs over the side of the bed. "We'd better go. Can't have people talking, can we?"

She tried to get off the bed, but Mark pulled her back, holding her close.

"Not until I've had me evil way with you, m'dear!" He chuckled softly. "You know, I have been fancying you all day."

"Oh, I thought it was Tracey you fancied." teased Kate, half-heartedly struggling to free herself from his embrace.

"Come here, wench!" he said, pulling her down beside him again. "And I'll show you who I fancy!"

৹ఎƠଷ

Later Mark waited as Kate repaired her make-up and tidied her hair.

"Do I look okay?" she asked turning to him with a radiant smile.

"Absolutely gorgeous," he said affectionately, then putting his hand on her shoulders, he kissed the tip of her nose.

"Happy, darling?" he asked.

"Very," she said, smiling up into his eyes. "It's been a perfect day. A perfect wedding."

"No worries? No fears?" he asked softly.

"None at all." Kate said happily. "I think Nick has done very well for himself. I thoroughly approve of Lisa, she's a lovely girl and will make a perfect wife for him."

"If she's half as good a wife as her mother-in-law, then Nick will be a very happy man indeed,"

Kate gave him a squeeze.

"Thank you, darling." she said happily. "I can't ask for more than that they are as happy as we are."

Mark quietly closed the hotel bedroom door, Kate slipped her arm through his and they walked down the stairs to join the rest of the guests who had gathered to celebrate the marriage of their only son, Nick, and his lovely bride Lisa.

LEOPARDS AND SPOTS

The morning sun shone on Danny's face, waking him from a deep sleep. He lay still, desperately trying to gather together his scattered memory of the night before.

His eye felt sore, he gingerly touched it, and his fingers discovered swollen tissue. He smiled as it all came flooding back to him.

He turned his head on the pillow and encountered the back of Clare, his pretty young wife, and he tentatively put a hand on the curve of her hip. She shrugged it off and moved farther away from him, so he put a hand over her shoulder and tried to pull her towards him. She moved to the edge of the bed and got up, saying nothing.

"Okay, babe?" he asked brightly.

Without replying she pulled on her housecoat, and left the room, banging the door behind her.

After a while Danny got out of bed and padded to the bathroom. He looked in the mirror and inspected his face closely. His usually good-looking face was marred by a swollen black eye.

He leaned closer to the mirror, and gently examined the purplish-red area with interest. He was relieved to see that the eye itself wasn't blood-shot, which meant that the injury was superficial and would soon heal.

Danny grinned at his reflection, winked, turned on the shower and stepped under the soothing warm water. As he soaped his body, he went over the events of the night before in his mind. It had been great!

Clare was pregnant and hadn't wanted to go out, so Danny had asked if she minded if he went out for a pint with his mates. Although not keen on the idea, she knew he would be rotten company if she asked him to stay in with her, so she had reluctantly agreed, pointing out that she expected him not to be late coming home. He had assured her that he would be home about eleven.

Danny and his group of friends had visited many pubs in the small town where they lived, and at closing time seven or eight very inebriated young men, including Danny (his promise to Clare forgotten), ended up at a poky little night club, where they could dance and drink until the small hours.

While they were drinking at the bar, Danny spotted, Sharon, a girl he knew by sight. She was flashily pretty, with blonde hair, a low cut top and a very short mini-skirt. Danny fancied her, although he thought she wasn't half as pretty as Clare.

He made his way over to where she stood alone at the bar, took her hand without a word and led her onto the crowded little dance floor. He wasn't too drunk to use his charm, and with his twinkling eyes and roguish repartee, he soon had her giggling. She even wrote her phone number on a scrap of paper and gave it to him. When he pulled her closer to him she didn't object to him nuzzling her neck as they smooched.

He was whispering seductively in her ear, when they were suddenly pulled apart, and Danny received a blow just above his eye from Steve, Sharon's irate boy friend, who had returned to the bar, to see her in Danny's embrace.

Steve immediately regretted his hasty action, because before he could land another punch, Danny had grabbed him and head-butted him on the nose, which made Steve cry out in pain. Then a swift punch to the head was quickly followed by another to the body, which sent him crashing to his knees. Danny, his temper now burning brightly, drew back his foot to deliver a kick to the hapless Steve, but his mates arrived on the scene and restrained him before he could inflict serious damage to the lad, who was already bleeding profusely from his nose.

A crowd gathered around baying for blood, but Danny and his mates were escorted from the club by the bouncers, and decided to leave fairly quietly, discretion being the better part of valour.

Once out in the night air and far enough away from the club, they were triumphant. They laughingly discussed the fight, recalling the feebleness of Steve's attack, the ferocity of Danny's retaliation and the look of surprise on Steve's face when Danny head-butted him.

Danny was elated. If there was anything he liked better than a few beers and chatting up a pretty chick, it was a good fight. To his mind this had been a perfect night out.

His mates were in awe of him, and his temper was legendary. It could flare up, burn brightly, and die within a minute, but while it burned, he was dangerous, and awesome to see.

Danny stepped from the shower and towelled himself down. He dressed in tee shirt and jeans, gelled and combed his hair into a spiky fashionable style. He examined his eye once more. It was looking quite impressive, though he doubted Clare would think so.

He bounded downstairs and into the kitchen. Clare was sitting at the table sipping coffee from a mug. He put his arm around her shoulders and kissed her cheek.

She shrugged him off and glared at him.

"You mad at me, babe?" he asked innocently.

She ignored him.

"I'm sorry I was late, babe." he continued. "But you know what the lads are like."

Clare scowled at him. "It was gone two when you got in." she said crossly. "And I see you've been fighting again, by the look of that eye."

"It wasn't my fault." Danny said defensively.

"It never is, is it?" she answered with a trace of sarcasm.

Suddenly, she let out all the pent up anger she had been holding back and yelled at him, her dark eyes blazing with fury.

"I was awake half the night, worried sick because you were so late, then once you were home, I was even more worried wondering what you'd been up to. It's not fair, Danny!"

Her anger turned to tears and great sobs racked her body, as she covered her face with her hands.

Danny put his arms round her, feeling guilty for making her so upset.

"I'm really sorry, babe." he said gently, stroking her hair and kissing her softly. "I honestly didn't mean to be late. I just didn't realise what the time was. You know what I'm like when I get with the lads. I was going to come home when the pub closed, but they wanted to go to the club. I would rather be home here with you, honest. It won't happen again, I promise."

Clare sniffed and dabbed her eyes with a tissue.

"You always say that." she sobbed. "But you don't mean it."

"I do this time, honest." he said aloud, but thought. "I always mean it when I say it."

Before long Danny's charm and sweet talking won Clare round, and she dried her eyes and was soon basking in the warmth of his loving attention. She could never be angry with him for long.

While she cooked their breakfast Danny entertained her with tales of his night out, suitably censored. She was soon laughing at his accounts of their antics, the jokes at the expense of friends and strangers alike, the people they met up with and gossip about the girls his mates were seeing, or had just dumped. Gradually, he built up his account of the fight in the night club.

He told her every detail, although he omitted to include Sharon's part in the proceedings, saying that it started because he jostled Steve at the bar.

"I wish you wouldn't fight." she said, examining his bruised eye. "One of these days you will get badly hurt."

"No chance!" he laughed confidently.

She shook her head and kissed him warmly.

"What am I going to do with you?"

"I have a few suggestions!" he laughed, with a naughty twinkle in his eye, happy that she was no longer annoyed with him.

After they had eaten he dutifully helped with the dishes, and tidied up their living room.

He would have loved to go and watch his local team play football, but decided not to push his luck now that Clare was sweet again, so they did the things she enjoyed doing; a bit of shopping, a short walk in the park, then a weepy film on TV. Boring stuff, but worth it to keep her happy, because in spite of everything, he did love her very much, and was looking forward to the birth of their first child.

The rest of the week end passed uneventfully, Clare was happy that he stayed in with her and they discussed painting the nursery and what names they would give their child, which was due in a couple of months.

On Monday Danny drove them both to work as usual. They worked for the same company, but in different departments. It was through work that they met, getting together at the annual outing and going steady for a year before they got married. It was a lovely wedding. The happiest day of Clare's twenty two years of life. Danny's family loved her and hoped married life would tame the wild streak in him. Her family were equally as fond of Danny. Their reservations about his wild side were soon banished by his charm and wit. Everyone thought that they made a perfect couple.

As they drove along the high street of their town Danny was alarmed to see Sharon waiting at the bus stop. She recognised him, beamed broadly and waved. Danny raised his hand without enthusiasm. She was wearing a black leather min-skirt, low top and high heeled sandals. Her fluffy blonde hair shone like a beacon in the bright morning sunshine.

"Who was that?" Clare asked suspiciously.

"She goes out with one of the lads, I think." Danny answered vaguely. "I don't really know her."

"Well, she seems to know you." Clare said sarcastically.

She sunk down in the seat with a sulky expression on her face, and they drove the rest of the way in silence.

When he parked the car, Danny gave Clare a peck on the cheek and they went their separate ways.

Soon Danny was relating the story of how he got his black eye to various colleagues. He altered the details slightly depending on his audience.

The young men listened with interest, wishing they had the same ability to charm girls and envying his strong physique. Some of the older men shook there heads disapprovingly, although they secretly admired the feisty young man.

As he walked to his work area he was gratified to see that his black eye was getting a lot of attention from the women and girls who worked on the shop floor. He smiled at the most attractive, keeping a wary eye out for Clare, who was already installed at her work station and chatting to her group of friends, whilst keeping a sharp look out for her wayward husband, making sure he wasn't giving too much attention to any one girl in particular. She hated it when he chatted and flirted with the young women, which was something he felt compelled to do.

Danny felt good when he got to his work area. He ignored the odd sarcastic remarks about his being late to get down to the job, offering everyone a cheery 'Good morning!'

Danny had a special sort of relationship with Janet, his supervisor. She was a middle-aged woman with daughters of her own, and she looked on Danny as the son she never had. She was broadminded and enjoyed his saucy sense of humour. He trusted her and often confided in her, especially about problems with Clare and her jealousy over other girls he came into contact with

When Janet saw his black eye, she winced.

"Now what have you been up to?" she asked with a sigh. He grinned and winked at her with his good eye.

"Brilliant week-end, Jan." he grinned. "You should have seen the other guy!"

"Mmm." she said in a non-committal way, and didn't ask him any questions, knowing that when the time was right he would tell her all about the events of the week-end.

Later in the day they worked together and Danny told her about the Saturday night fight and the events that led up to it. She was the only one whom he trusted enough to tell the whole story to.

"That Sharon's a bit tasty, Jan." he said with a grin, adding. "I was doing all right with her until that prat Steve interfered. Still, she is often at the club, so I can try again another time. She looked pleased to see me this morning when we passed her at the bus stop."

"You are incorrigible, Danny!" Janet said shaking her head.

He grinned at her, his green eyes sparkling with mischief.

"I know I am!" he agreed. "But it's all part of my charm, right?"

"One of these days you are going to get into real trouble, and the famous charm won't help you then." Janet warned.

Danny shrugged and went off to work in another area.

One of the reasons that Janet found Danny so interesting was his multi-layered personality. One minute he was charming and thoughtful, then in an instant he could become angry, foul-mouthed and insulting. This could be very hurtful at times, but he was never dull. He was intelligent, of that there was no doubt and when he was calm, he was sensible and a good worker. She did worry about him, because his mercurial personality could get him into all kinds of scrapes. Janet hoped that marriage to the sweet-natured Clare, and the birth of their child might be the calming influence he needed to buckle down. However, the events of the week-end proved that he still had a long way to go.

At coffee break Danny went off to see Clare. When he returned Janet could see that he looked worried.

"OK?" she asked.

Danny grunted, but said nothing.

"What's wrong?" she asked. "Has someone annoyed you?"

"Leave me alone, will you." he said crossly.

Janet shrugged and got on with her work, there was no point in trying to talk to him until he wanted to confide in her, which he would she knew, in his own time.

After the lunch break Danny, still looking worried, came and put a hand on Janet's shoulder.

"Sorry I snapped, Jan." he said softly. "Is it all right if I talk to you about something."

"Of course it is," she answered with a smile.

He told her that he had gone to see Clare at morning coffee break, worried because whenever he caught her eye throughout the morning, she had glared angrily at him, and as he'd approached her, she had turned her back on him. He had tried desperately to think of what he could have done to annoy her again, but could think of nothing.

When he sat down next to her in the canteen she had turned to him with a cold expression.

"Who is Sharon?" she demanded.

Danny had been a bit taken aback by the bluntness of the question, but tried to keep his face expressionless.

"Sharon?" he asked innocently. "Sharon who?"

"Don't give me that, Danny!" she snapped. "You know who I am talking about. The Sharon you were pawing about at the club on Saturday night."

Danny's heart had skipped a beat, and Clare, her eyes brimming with tears had turned her back and refused to discuss it anymore.

"I can tell you, Jan, I was shocked that she had found out about that Sharon episode. All morning I was trying to think up a plausible story to tell Clare about it, but since I didn't know how much she knew, I didn't really know what to say."

At lunchtime, when they usually ate in the canteen together, Clare had asked Danny to join her in their car, so they could talk in private.

Once settled, Clare, still angry, questioned Danny closely about his Saturday night adventure.

At first Danny denied that he had danced with any girls, but Clare had turned to him, even more angry than before.

"Don't lie to me, Danny!" she yelled, almost incandescent with rage. "You were seen, and the fight was over that slag Sharon, wasn't it? Go on, admit it. Tell me the truth for once!"

"OK, babe," Danny said quietly. "I admit I danced with her, but that is all. I was just being friendly. I told you when we saw her this morning, that she was with one of the lads."

"Hah!" Clare snorted angrily. "So that's who that was at the bus stop, was it? No wonder she recognised you." She drew a deep breath and continued. "And since when has Steve Jones been a mate of yours? And for your information, she isn't seeing him anymore. It seems they had a row on Saturday night, because she let some bloke paw her about on the dance floor. Now I wonder who that could have been?"

Danny looked perplexed.

"How come you know all this?" he asked, unable to contain his curiosity any longer.

"You really should be more careful what you do when you are out." snapped Clare. "After all, we live in a small town, and I do have a lot of friends."

"Yeah," Danny said sarcastically. "Real good friends who like telling tales and stirring up trouble it seems."

He began to get angry then, He hated to think he was being spied upon by someone who reported back to Clare.

"Go on then," he demanded. "Tell me who told you all this load of rubbish."

At first Clare was reluctant to tell him who had talked to her about

Danny's night out, but he finally managed to drag it out of her, and he was soon telling Janet the whole story.

Lisa, a girl who worked with Clare, was going out with Sharon's brother Jason and the couple had been with Steve and Sharon at the night club on Saturday night.

After the fuss and fight was over, the four of them had gone back to Lisa's flat to help Steve clean up his bloody nose. It wasn't broken, so a hospital visit was deemed unnecessary. After a while there had been a terrible row between Sharon and Steve over the way she seemed to enjoy dancing closely with Danny. He had threatened Sharon and her brother Jason had stepped in to protect his sister, and when Steve calmed down Jason had escorted him home, leaving the two girls alone.

Over a cup of coffee, Sharon told Lisa that she was going to finish with Steve, because she really fancied Danny, and was sure that the feeling was mutual.

"You know he's married, don't you?" Lisa had told her.

"A happily married man doesn't say the things to a girl that Danny said to me tonight." Sharon had told her smugly. "He obviously isn't with his wife anymore. He more or less told me as much and wants to see me again."

When Lisa got to work on Monday she had asked Clare when she and Danny had split up. Naturally, Clare was shocked to be asked such a thing.

"Whatever makes you think Danny and I aren't together anymore?" she asked in amazement.

Lisa had blushed with embarrassment and said she would say no more, but Clare insisted that if those sort of rumours were being circulated, then she had a right to know exactly what was being said.

Lisa then told her everything she knew, salving her conscience about telling tales by reasoning that Clare ought to know if Danny were misbehaving.

When Danny had finished telling Janet the story, she looked at him sternly.

"Did you say those things to Sharon?" she asked.

"Of course I didn't." he said, quickly adding "Well, I suppose I might have done, but I was drunk."

"And are you going to see her again?"

"Not now, I'm not!" Danny said fiercely. "Fancy the silly cow telling everyone what I said to her. Bloody Hell, it was only a bit of a chat up, She must have known I didn't mean it." Then giving Janet his cheekiest grin said "The old chat-up lines still work though, don't they Jan? She must really fancy me!" He laughed and added "And who can blame her?"

Janet ignored the remark.

"How's Clare now?" she asked.

"She won't talk to me." he said in a sulky way. "She believes that stupid Lisa's tale. Surely she must know that it is her I love. She's the one I married. The one whose having our baby."

"Perhaps you should remember that too." Janet said pointedly.

Danny had the good grace to look a little shame faced, but said nothing.

When work was over for the day, Danny laughed as Janet wished him good luck.

"She'll be Ok," he said with confidence. "I'll be extra nice to her tonight, and she'll realise that she's making a fuss over nothing. She'll soon get over it."

But she didn't.

They drove home in silence. Clare stared out of the window, completely ignoring Danny's presence in the car.

Danny's heart skipped a beat when he saw Sharon crossing the High Street. She smiled and waved, but both Danny and Clare ignored her.

Immediately the car stopped outside their house, Clare got out and instead of going into the kitchen to prepare their meal, as was her usual habit, she went upstairs and into their bedroom.

Danny saw that she was getting undressed, and taking this for an invitation, he went to embrace her, but she glared at him and pushed him away.

"Don't you dare touch me!" she snapped

She went into the bathroom, slammed and locked the door and then Danny heard the shower running, so he went downstairs and switched on the TV, and sprawled in a chair, watching the flickering screen without interest.

After a while, Clare came into the room. She looked lovely. She was wearing her prettiest dress and had obviously spent some time with her make up. He caught a whiff of the expensive perfume he had bought for her birthday. She ignored Danny's complimentary remarks, picked up her handbag and car keys and headed for the door.

"Where are you going?" asked Danny.

"Out!" she snapped, and swept out of the house, slamming the door behind her.

Danny heard her start the car and watched from the window as she drove away.

He sat down in front of the TV again, wondering what to do. He found the scrap of paper with Sharon's phone number, and wondered if he should give her a call. The idea appealed, but he thought it was wiser not to at the moment.

He considered going out for a pint, thinking he might see the lads and have a laugh about Saturday night's events, but then he realised that he didn't have any money, so he slumped in his chair, half watching the soap that Clare loved to watch.

"She must be really fed up with me to go out and miss this," he thought to himself. "I wonder where she's gone. She's all dolled up, so she hasn't just gone round to her mum's."

The more he thought about the situation the more annoyed he became. He admitted to himself that she had good reason to be cross with him, but felt she had taken things too far.

"After all," he said aloud. "What have I done? Nothing except talk to some girl. Clare can be so jealous and unreasonable at times."

He was really hungry now and looked at the clock. She had been gone an hour, no wonder he was starving. He went into the kitchen, looked in the fridge and decided to fry up some eggs and bacon.

He had just put the frying pan on the stove when the door bell rang.

"Aha!" he thought. "She must have forgotten her house keys."

He waited a while, not wanting to appear too eager, then slowly made his way to the front door, just as the bell rang again. He was trying to think of a suitably caustic remark to greet her with when he opened the door.

He was surprised and alarmed to see two policemen standing on the door step

"Mr. Rhodes?" one of them asked.

Danny nodded, thinking that Steve must have reported him for injuring him on Saturday.

"I'm afraid we have some rather bad news for you, sir." said one of the constables. "I'm afraid your wife has been involved in an accident."

Danny felt the colour drain from his face.

"She's not badly hurt, sir, but she is in hospital. Would you like us to take you there?"

Danny nodded again. He was visibly shaken. He grabbed his jacket and climbed into the back of the police car.

On the way to the hospital they told him that Clare had skidded on some mud in a country lane not far from their house, and turned the car over.

"By the state of the car, mate, she's lucky to be alive." said one of the policemen seriously. " A narrow escape for sure."

Almost before the car stopped outside the hospital, Danny was out and racing towards Accident & Emergency Unit. The receptionist directed him to the ward that Clare was in and he ran along the corridors, his heart racing.

He entered the ward and told the young nurse on the desk who he was.

She smiled at him reassuringly.

"Don't look so worried, Mr. Rhodes, you wife is OK. She is very shocked and shaken, but she is unhurt, apart from a little bruising. The baby is fine too, but we want to keep her in for twenty four hours for observation, just in case, but there is no reason why she can't go home tomorrow evening."

"That's great." Danny said, the relief written all over his face. "I'll pick her up after I finish work tomorrow evening. Can I see her now?"

"Of course," she said with a gentle smile. "But don't stay too long, she is very tired and needs to rest."

She pointed out Clare's bed to him, then laid a cool hand on his arm.

"She'll be as right as rain in next to no time."

"Thanks." Danny smiled at her gratefully and made his way to Clare's bed.

As he approached he saw Clare lying with her eyes closed. She looked so pale and still that his heart went out to her. He took her hand in his.

"Hello, Babe." he said softly.

Clare opened her eyes, sat up and threw her arms tightly round his neck and began to weep against his shoulder.

"Oh, Danny!" she sobbed. "I think the car's a write-off, and it's all my fault."

"Never mind the car." Danny said sincerely. "That's only a lump of metal. It's you that I am worried about."

"I have been so stupid." she whispered shakily. "I could have killed our baby."

Danny dried her tears.

"But you didn't, so there's no need to go upsetting yourself. You just relax and get some sleep and tomorrow you can come home with me and everything will be fine."

Clare calmed down, and lay back against the pillows, looking exhausted.

"Listen," Danny said softly, as he gently squeezed her hand. "I'm really sorry about all that business with Sharon. She means nothing to me, honest. All I want is you and our baby. I'll prove it to you when you get home. I promise I won't go out without you ever again."

He realised that this was a rather rash statement, but he was relying on Clare's sweet nature to come to his rescue, and she didn't let him down.

"Don't be silly, Danny." she said with a warm smile. "I really don't mind you going out with your mates occasionally."

"Well, OK then, just one night a week." he said trying not to sound too relieved.

He bent to kiss her, and she put her arms round his neck again.

"I do trust you really." she said. "But I just can't help getting jealous when I think you want other women. I am just scared of losing you."

"Now why would I want to go off with some cheap little blonde, when I have the most beautiful girl in the world at home/"

Clare glowed with pleasure at Danny's compliment, smiled contentedly and settled back on her pillows.

Danny kissed her fondly and stroked the dark hair back from her forehead.

"You go to sleep now, Babe, and I'll come and fetch you tomorrow night after work. Night, Babe. I love you."

"I love you too," Clare whispered.

She watched him as he left the ward. His tall straight back, strong physique and boyish charm made her so proud that Danny loved and wanted her. She almost felt sorry for Sharon, because she couldn't have him.

Soon Clare drifted off to sleep, to dream of her and Danny with their baby living happily ever after.

The next day Danny felt on top of the world. Everything had turned out well for him. It was a nuisance not having a car to go to work in, but he managed to get a lift with a friend. The insurance would pay out and all would be well again.

The Sharon problem seemed to be solved. At least Clare was now satisfied that he had no desire to have anything more to do with Sharon and as long as the girl didn't keep pestering him, it should all be fine. He made up his mind that if he saw her when he was out with his mates, he would just take her to one side and have a quiet word with her. He would explain that he had no intention of ever leaving Clare, and see how things went from there.

When he got to work Danny told Janet all about the traumatic events of the night before. She listened in silence until he had told her everything.

"Thank goodness Clare's all right." she said when he had finished his tale. "And the baby. Poor Clare, what a rotten thing to happen after the horrible day she had been through."

"What about me?" Danny asked petulantly. "My day wasn't all that good either. I even had to cook my own supper."

He looked serious for a moment.

""I was really scared, Jan." he said. "It made me realise just how much Clare means to me when I thought I might have lost her."

"Good," said Janet. "I hope this means that you have learned a lesson and stop playing with fire."

"Too right," he said with a frown. "I have."

"I'm pleased to hear it." Janet gave him a quick hug. "It's about time."

Suddenly, Danny gave her a great grin and his green eyes sparkled.

"I'll tell you what though." he said. "That nurse was a bit tasty. I reckon she fancied me. She kept smiling at me, and she put her hand on my arm too, She was really nice. I wonder if she will be there tonight when I pick Clare up." He grinned broadly. "I will have to look out for her. She's about twenty two, blonde, slim, nice boobs and much prettier than Sharon. What do you reckon, Jan?"

Janet just sighed and shook her head.

"Leopards and spots come to mind." she said.

FIRST
DAY BACK (1)

The Writer's group set an exercise to write a piece entitled First Day Back. I wrote two. Both stories are in this book.

Alice woke to find the sun shining across the bedroom floor and gathering in a pool on her pillow. She turned over and tried to go back to sleep, but she couldn't shake off the feeling of dread that had kept her awake until the early hours.

She glanced at the clock. Almost six and far too early to get up. Neil was sleeping like a baby. No disturbing thoughts were keeping him awake.

Resigning herself to not going back to sleep, she let her mind run free, and she thought about the holiday they had just enjoyed. It had been wonderful!

How she loved Italy. The sunshine, the glorious scenery, the warm, happy people, and of course, the delicious food.

Sorrento was so beautiful. Each morning after breakfast they wandered from their hotel, strolling through the cobbled streets, enjoying the sights and sounds. They stopped to buy fruit, fresh crusty bread and tomatoes, ripe and warm from the sun. A piece of local cheese and a bottle of wine completed their purchases, which they took back to the hotel to eat on the balcony at lunch time. When replete they took their siesta, lying on the cool bed drowsy and content.

Later they would get showered and dressed and wander through the crowded streets, still warm in the evening sunshine. A drink in a pavement café, where they could people-watch, passed the time until dinner.

They would choose a different restaurant each night the first week, returning to those they had particularly enjoyed during the second week.

Some afternoons they strolled down to the Piccola Marina, where refreshed by a rich and creamy gelata on the way, they would watch the fishermen mending their nets, while beautiful dark-eyed children paddled in the shallow water, their laughter and rapid chatter filling the air with joy.

After climbing the steep steps back to the town, they would stop for a cappuccino, frothy as sea-foam, with a dusting of powdered chocolate or cinnamon on top.

One day they hired a car and drove along the coast to Amalfi. "The most beautiful road in the world" the guide book said, and they believed it. The scenery was breath-taking. To their left the mountain climbed rugged, craggy and noisy with the sound of cicadas, and to the right the Mediterranean, glittering like cobalt glass beneath the deep blue sky. With each bend in the road, there was another stunning vista.

They pulled over into a viewing point and looking over a low wall they saw the little resort of Positano shimmering in the heat below them. Bougainvillea scrambled in a riot of purple, magenta and pink over the walls of the buildings, that looked from that distance like dolls houses, while splashes of scarlet geraniums pinpointed piazzas and balconies. Toy-sized boats bobbed in the sparkling waters of the harbour. It was all so beautiful.

They bought ice-cold lemon-sodas at a way-side stall and sipped them as they marvelled at the stunning view.

Amalfi was everything they had hoped. It's ancient and lovely old cathedral, shops and view of the Saracen tower, taking their breath away.

After looking round the town they found a small, but attractive ristorante and enjoyed a delicious lunch of zuppa di pesce, a fragrant fish, tomato and garlic soup, served with crisp panini that they used to mop up their bowls.

Afterwards they had driven up the mountain to Ravello, where the famous gardens over-look the sea, many miles below. In the honey-gold light the bee-filled flowers nodded lazily. The colours of the cannas, geraniums and gazanias were intensified by the mellow warmth of the afternoon sun.

They had been so enchanted by everything they saw, that they stayed until the gardens closed, watching the sea turn from sapphire to amethyst as the sun went down.

To refresh themselves before their drive back down the mountain they sat at a pavement café in the wide piazza and enjoyed a cassata, a rich ice cream concoction, stuffed with fruit and nuts, that only the Italians can make to perfection.

Now, lying in bed, Alice remembered it all. They had been home for only two days, but it all seemed so long ago and far away now.

She looked at the clock again. Still only six fifteen.

"What were we doing last Monday?" she thought.

Ah yes, that was the day they went to Pompeii. Truly one of the wonders of the world. It had been so hot! The excavated city baked in the sun beneath the slumbering Vesuvius, looking much as it had done two thousand years ago. Incredible streets of shops lining roads that had stepping stones in order to cross safely. These stones were set to allow a chariots wheels to pass between them. Then there was the grand villa that had a mosaic tile at its entrance saying "Cave Cane!" (beware of the dog). So many little things to make one realise that real people had lived here, before the city disappeared under a suffocating blanket of volcanic dust.

The place was amazing and they spent several hours wandering round on their own, refusing to accept the offer of a guide, preferring to move round at their own pace.

Because of the heat they stopped for drinks on several occasions. As well as water, they enjoyed the sharp tasting lemonade that was on sale.

When they left the historic site they found a restaurant and enjoyed a memorable meal of tortellini in a rich cream and basil sauce, liberally sprinkled with Parmesan cheese, served with a crisp salad and a bottle of Lagrima Cristi (tears of Christ) a local white wine made from grapes grown on the slopes of Vesuvius.

Alice then recalled the trip across the Bay of Naples to Capri, where they visited the Blue Grotto and gasped in surprise and wonder when they entered the cave in a hired rowing boat . The boatman splashed his oar in the water sending a spectacular shower of glittering sapphire-like droplets into the eerie light of the grotto.

Lunch on the island was a simple dish of spaghetti, with tomatoes, garlic and herbs, although Alice couldn't resist the tiramasu, which was sweet and creamy and utterly decadent.

Both she and Neil were exhilarated by the chair lift up to Ana Capri, the highest part of the island. It was here that Tiberius had a palace and would throw bringers of bad news over the wall and onto the rocks below.

The little café here was expensive, but the view was breathtaking, so worth very lira spent of cappuccino and pastries.

Alice remembered the food again. Such a diverse selection of wonderful flavours; pasta in all it's forms, sea food, tender meat, risottos, salads and delicious breads dipped in fragrant olive oil. Then there were the cheeses, succulent plum shaped tomatoes and a variety of juicy fruits. It had all been utterly delicious

Alice longed for the bunches of sun-warmed grapes, apricots, nectarines and peaches, that they bought from one of the fruit stalls in the market. Sainsbury's fruit and veg section just wasn't the same as bargaining with the handsome black-eyed boy who flirted wit h her as she selected the produce from his stall. She even enjoyed Neil's little jealous jibes as she glowed with pleasure at the boy's compliments.

Alice looked at the clock. It was seven now, so she got up and went into the kitchen to make coffee. She heard Neil taking his shower and in a few minutes he joined her.

"Ah well," he said tying his shoe laces. "Back to work today. Before long it will seem like I've never been away. The first day back is the worst."

Alice silently poured his coffee and buttered his toast.

"Why so glum, darling?" He said, as Alice morosely munched on her muesli. "Pining for your beloved Italy? Cheer up, we can always go back next year." He chuckled. "Or is it Tino your little greengrocer boy you're missing? He's probably chatting up some other gullible English lady now."

Alice shot him a cold look.

"It's not that." She said crossly, then sighed. ""It's just that after two weeks of utter indulgence, today is my first day back at Weight Watchers."

FIRST
DAY BACK (2)

A tap on the bedroom door dragged me from a fitful sleep.

"Come in." I called sleepily.

"Good morning, Lucy."

Mum placed a cup of tea on my bedside table, kissed me on the forehead and strode across the room to throw back the curtains, letting the mellow September sunshine spill across the carpet and on onto my pillow.

"It's a beautiful day." she said brightly.

"No it isn't." I grumbled, pulling the bedclothes over my head. "How can it be beautiful? It's my first day back at school. Ugh!"

"Let's hear no more of that sort of talk," Mum said briskly. "Come on, it's gone seven and breakfast will be ready in half an hour."

"I don't want any breakfast." I said sulkily. "I couldn't eat a thing."

"Of course you want breakfast! You can't go out with an empty stomach." Mum insisted. "We don't want you passing out in assembly, do we?"

"We don't have assembly anymore." I muttered.

"Huh, no wonder children are so badly behaved these days," Mum sniffed and marched out of the room and down the stairs to prepare something nourishing. "Half an hour. OK?" she called from the hallway.

"OK," I confirmed without enthusiasm.

I drank the tea, then climbed out of bed, wandered over to the window and gazed out into the garden. It still looked like summer, even though the parched lawn was sprouting a few green blades after the recent rain. The bedding plants looked tired, the roses over-blown and the chestnut tree, that only a few short months ago glowed with glorious floral candles, was looking decidedly autumnal, its large leaves already turning a russet brown. It all looked as melancholy as I felt.

"School," I sniffed, dangerously close to tears. "Why can't summer last forever."

෨෬

My summer had been wonderful! I had gone to stay with my best friend Judy and her family in their villa in Tuscany, where the days drifted by in a golden haze of sunshine, good company and wonderful

Italian food. Most days Judy and I swam in their pool, often accompanied by her brother James, or we wandered round the village. Occasionally we took a bus into the nearby town to shop and spoil ourselves with delicious ice creams. The delights of homework far from our minds as we relished the joys of our slothful lifestyle.

Judy's parents were wealthy, charming and generous, making me feel so welcome, that I was completely at home in their sumptuous villa for almost all of the school holiday.

Judy, James and I made friends with an Italian boy from the village, Marco, who was about the same age as us, and the four of us spent almost every day together, swimming, laughing and generally enjoying the relaxed atmosphere of the wonderful Italian countryside. It was perfect.

James was a few years older than us, and was so funny, attentive and achingly handsome that I fell madly in love with him the moment we met.

His sun-bleached hair, lean bronzed torso and sophisticated air made him irresistible. He was always immaculately turned out in expensive designer label casual clothes, which enhanced his good looks. I had never known anyone like him before and my feelings got the better of me. Oh, I had had some school girl crushes, but this was different. He made me feel grown up. He was always charming and made me feel so special, that I was sure he liked me as much as I liked him.

The last night of my stay at the villa James and I walked hand in hand together in the garden after everyone else had gone to bed. The moon was full and the scent of jasmine filled the warm night air. We stopped beneath a pergola covered with roses and he turned to face me.

"Come here, Funny-Face," He said quietly, pulled me gently into his arms and kissed me softly on the lips. I wound my arms round his neck and returned his kisses passionately, moaning slightly with the unexpected delight of the moment.

"Whoa!" He said gently, pulling away slightly. "We had better go in I think." and without further explanation he took my hand and led me back into the villa, where he kissed me softly on the cheek.

"Good night, sweet little Lucy," he whispered. "Maybe we can pick up where we left off next year, but right now I think we should say good-night." He smiled his dazzling smile and added. "You are very pretty, but I am not into baby-snatching." He turned on his heel and was gone, leaving me feeling like a child, hurt and disappointed, with tears blurring my vision.

The next morning he was gone before I got up, but there was a note by my breakfast plate. I didn't open it at once, but took it to me room to read in private.

"Sweet Funny-Face," I read. "Don't be sad and cry. Remember the fun we had and be happy. Maybe I'll see you at Ma and Pa's at Christmas, if not, then here next year, although you may well have found yourself someone special by then. Who knows? Whatever happens, I'll never forget you.

Love J xx."

Judy poked her head round the door.

"Are you OK, Lucy?" she asked, her pretty face full of concern.

I showed her the note and collapsed in floods of tears.

"Fun!" I wailed. "It wasn't just fun. It was wonderful, romantic and very special. I adore him!"

"Oh dear, poor Lucy," Judy wrapped her arms around me. "Not you too? Every single one of my friends falls for James. He is such a charmer. He can't help it, you know."

"But he kissed me, " I sighed, then drying my eyes on a tissue I said "I know what I'll do, I'll write to him. That's it, you can give me his phone number and e-mail address, or even the address of his flat in London, can't you?"

"I suppose I can," Judy sounded uncertain. "But really, I wouldn't bother if I were you. He is terrible at keeping in touch. Ma is always nagging him about it." She looked serious. "Honestly Lucy, he isn't worth getting upset about. He has girl friends all over the place. We can never keep up with them." She squeezed my hand. "And to be brutally honest, he prefers older, more sophisticated women. His latest was a divorcee in her late thirties. He means well, he really does, but he was simply enjoying your company while he was here. His stay at the villa was really a duty thing, you know, to please Ma and Pa by spending some time with them, and to have an adoring female around made it all the more pleasant for him. He wasn't being serious. Believe me, I know my brother."

"He said he'd see me at Christmas, or maybe here next year." I whispered, blowing my nose.

"Then he probably will." Judy jumped off the bed, and sounding impatient with me she added, "But I wouldn't hold my breath. Come on, let's pack, then I have to pop down to the village to say good bye to Marco."

ಸಂಗ

I had been home from Italy for a week, and I still couldn't get James off my mind. Now I was going back to school, where the new term stretched ahead like a never ending road. I couldn't bear it!

I showered and dressed and wandered downstairs into the kitchen where Mum was scrambling eggs and making toast. I poured myself a cup of coffee and sat at the table morosely sipping it, my mood as black as the liquid in the cup.

"Do cheer up, Lucy!" Mum said brightly, placing the perfectly cooked eggs and golden toast before me. "It can't be that bad, surely. I thought you liked school."

"I did when I was sixteen. " I sighed. "Life was less complicated then, but now …" My voice trailed off.

"But last term you were full of ideas and enthusiasm and you couldn't wait to go back. What's so different now?"

"Everything," I sighed. "The classes are too big, there's trouble with bullying, most of the teachers are disillusioned and worry about violence, exam results and league tables, but for me the worst thing of all is that Judy has left. I could face anything when she was around, but now …"

"You'll soon make new friends, dear," Mum said sympathetically, topping up my coffee cup. "Now eat your breakfast. I won't take no for an answer."

I forced a little of the food down and looked at the clock.

"Time I left." I said getting up and kissing Mum on the cheek. "Thanks, breakfast was great."

"Have a good day, " she said as I left, then patting my bottom she added. "It will be all right, you'll see."

ఌఌ

A feeling of dread swept over me as I entered the school. It was well before nine, so there were only a few early birds about, people like me, who were nervous about the new school year and the work load.

I entered my new class room and opened my desk, sorting through my work and preparing myself mentally for the day ahead. All thoughts of Italy and James were pushed to the back of my mind, I had to concentrate on the here and now.

All too soon a noisy hubbub filled the room and I swallowed a feeling of panic, before looking up to see a sea of shiny, eager faces gazing intently in my direction.

I stood up and cleared my throat.

"Good morning, everyone." I said firmly, with hardly any tremor at all in my voice.

"Good morning, Miss Richards." my new class answered in unison.

Bouquet

(This poem was written for my four nieces Louise, Amanda, JoAnne and Sarah When they were teenagers in 1985)

I have four nieces in their teens
Each one a precious pearl
Folk ask me "Whose the prettiest?
Which one's your favourite girl?"

My answer to these questions
Has always been the same
How can I differentiate?
They all deserve acclaim.

What flower in the garden
Is more lovely than the rest?
Each in its way is perfect
Not one of them is best.

Bouquet (Continued)

Can you compare the waxen lily
And its heady sweet perfume
With the delicate scent of rose buds
Or the sweet peas fragile bloom

Take the fiery red geranium
Or the snowdrops cooler tone
Each in its turn gives pleasure
Each has beauty of its own.

All my nieces give me pleasure
Each in her separate way.
And a sweeter bunch of blossoms
Never brightened any day.

A SANGUINE AFFAIR

"Who is that beautiful girl in white?" Prince Rufus asked his equerry.

"She is the Countess Clara du Primeva, your highness."

"Where is she from?"

"It is her father's castle that we passed on our journey here, your highness."

"I wish to dance with her. Bring her to me, please."

"At once, your highness."

The equerry was soon back with the girl, who curtsied low, her eyes demurely lowered.

Rufus had never seen anyone as beautiful. Her oval face was as pale and perfect as a cameo. Her black hair fell into thick glossy ringlets around her creamy shoulders, and was fastened by a blood red rose. Her dark brows and crimson lips were a startling contrast to the paleness of her skin.

"You wish to dance with me, your highness?" she said softly, her voice as warm as a summers day.

"Indeed I do, my lady." Rufus replied, holding out his arms to her.

She melted into them and his heart beat faster.

They danced every dance from then on. Rufus was enchanted by her beauty, wit and intelligence.

The time flew by so quickly that Rufus was distressed when Clara whispered in his ear.

"Sir, I have to leave. My father expects me home by dawn."

"I cannot bear to let you go until I know when I can see you again." cried Rufus, pressing her white hand to his lips.

"I know not when that will be." she said softly, then added. "Sir, pray do not think me bold, but you could ride with me in my carriage to my father's castle. We would be alone, and who knows what might occur."

Rufus needed no more persuasion and agreed to accompany her.

After she had collected her cloak, they were soon ensconced in her carriage and fell into each other's arms at once, as they were driven slowly along the highway.

"Oh, my sweet prince." Clara sighed, as Rufus rained kisses on her face. "You are the most handsome man I have ever met."

"And you, Clara, are everything I ever wanted in a woman."

He slid an arm around her and drew her even closer. A shaft of moonlight caught her face, making her black eyes glitter like jet. Her skin had the sheen of the moonlight itself and the soft red lips parted to reveal gleaming white teeth. Rufus was besotted.

He moved into her embrace and his mouth sought hers, eager to feel the touch of her lips on his, but with a deft movement she avoided his kiss and sank her sharp little teeth into his neck and drank deeply, until Rufus was an empty shell..

When she was replete, she wiped her mouth delicately on the back of her hand.

"Daddy said I would enjoy blue blood." Smiled the beautiful Clara du Primeva, daughter of Count Dracula. "And he was right!"

೮೦ಌ

Note: If Rufus had been good at anagrams, he might have escaped unhurt! Clara du Primeva or …?

MY PEOPLE NEXT DOOR
(A True Story)

The first thing I have to point out is that of my many assets, my adorableness is the greatest. You don't believe me? Come on, just take a look. How could you doubt it?

Look at my big blue eyes, my silky cream fur, appealing face with a cute little nose and all over fluffiness. My little ears are neat and so striking in the rich chocolate brown fur that covers them. My legs are the same delightful shade, ending in dainty little white toes, that some say are my best feature, but I think my gorgeous chocolate brown tail is my prize possession. All in all I am a very handsome creature.

I keep all these remarkable assets in tip top condition by constant grooming. This is very necessary, because my people will insist on touching me all the time, understandable of course, but one never knows where they have been, does one?

The first people I decided to own were a family of four. They think they chose me, poor deluded souls, but it was me who made the choice. They are OK. The adults seem to behave themselves quite well. She feeds me and he makes sure that I am let in at night (when I want to be) and I allow them to stroke me from time to time. The children like to play with me. When I was a kitten and didn't know any better, I put up with it. I could understand why they wanted to hold me all the time. I was the sweetest little bundle of fluff you ever saw, at least that is what they used to say about me. I quite liked being petted, but then, after a while, I would want to be left alone, so I soon cured them of handling me when I wasn't in the mood. A quick nip with my needle sharp teeth, or a rake across the hand with my sharp little claws and they soon dropped me.

This family of mine are usually out all day, so I am often left alone. I like a bit of company sometimes, so began to look for people to own when mine are away.

It was a nice bright day around Christmas that I first noticed her and thought she looked as if she would do nicely. She lived next door to me, so I wouldn't have to go far to tame her. Admittedly, she was a bit of a challenge, but then nothing is fun if it is too easy.

I watched from under the hedge as she hung out her laundry. Louis, the cat from the house the other side of hers, strolled by, minding his own business. She hissed at him in a most unseemly manner, so that the poor fellow was scared half to death and ran into the bushes. I had seen her do this to every cat in the neighbourhood who dared venture into her precious garden. She was quite ruthless.

I couldn't understand why she did this, but on observing her for a while I decided that it was because she likes birds. So do I as a matter of fact, but she likes to see them feeding from the seed containers she hangs in the trees, and the bread she throws out on the lawn. I prefer to eat them, or at least play with them for a while after I have stalked them and hunted them down.

I assumed from this unseemly behaviour that she didn't like cats, so winning her over was going to be a challenge and more difficult than I first thought, but I was sure I could do it.

One day I saw her in the garden and squeezed through the hedge and casually strolled over to the bowl of water she puts out for her beloved birds. This water is delicious! The blackbirds, robins and thrushes bathe in it and it tastes tantalisingly of all three, with a dash of wren and chaffinch to add a little zest.

Seeing me lapping at the water, she started hissing and yelling at me to go away. A most undignified performance I must say. However, from my study of her, I was pretty sure that she wasn't likely to use violence , so I trotted up to her, blinked my blue eyes in a most subservient and docile way, rubbing round her legs and mewing softly.

That really surprised her and caught her off guard. She stooped down to stroke me.

"You're a pretty little puss." She exclaimed.

Pretty indeed ! Handsome maybe, beautiful and royal, most certainly, for I am an aristocrat, but pretty? Not a word I would have chosen.

I allowed her to caress my back and put up with her cooing over me as she did so. A small price to pay for ingratiating myself with her.

It took a while, but every day I went to see her and allowed a little more intimacy each time, until I had her eating out of my paw, or more importantly, me eating out of hers!

She eventually allowed me into her kitchen. She firmly shut the door to the rest of the house, but this was a great breakthrough, for it was in the kitchen that she prepared their meals and she gave me little tit-bits of the most delicious kind. There was, however, a price to be paid for this, for I had to do things that makes me cringe to think about it! For instance, she loved to see me roll over and tap her foot with my toes. For some reason this made her speak in a ridiculous voice.

"Just look at those pretty little white toes." She would squeak. "Aren't they the cutest things you ever saw/"

Well, yes, they are and I suppose it was nice of her to say so, but it's so embarrassing when she says it in baby-talk.

"Does the little pussy-cat have a name?" She asked me one day.

What a stupid question! Of course I have a name. Doesn't everyone? The trouble is she couldn't pronounce it even if I told her. Even my own people can't speak Burmese, so they call me Chester, which is not at all like my aristocratic name, but since I seldom take any notice when they call me, it doesn't really matter anyway.

One day she actually picked me up. This surprised and worried me at first, because I thought she might hurt me, but she was quite gentle and only tickled my ears and told me how beautiful I was. I have to admit that I quite liked it, but I didn't want her getting too familiar and taking liberties, so after a while I scratched her and she put me down.

My one ambition was to get into the rest of the house, so one day I slid past her and sat by the living room fire, grooming myself. She dashed over to me when she realised that I was in and was about to throw me out, when I played one of my 'cute' cards. I rolled over and tapped her foot with my toes, purring loudly.

She softened at once.

"You are so adorable!" She said, scooping me up into her arms. "How can I possibly resist you?"

From then on it was easy. I called on her every day, especially when I could smell cooking, because then I was sure of getting delicious little offerings from her. She soon learned that I didn't like my food mucked about with. You can keep your fancy sauces and gravies. I like my fish and meat served plain and simple.

I soon discovered that she thought it was really cute when I stood on my hind legs, reached up with my paws and scooped little scraps of food she placed for me on the edge of the counter. This is tedious and hard work, but it's a small price to pay for an extra little piece of steak or salmon.

She talks to me all the time and even asks me questions. I wouldn't bother to answer her idiotic queries even if I could, so I just try and ignore it as best I can and she doesn't realise, poor soul.

One day she had the temerity to tickle my tummy. I have a very nice tummy, all creamy silken fur and I am sure it is irresistible, but I do not allow anyone to tickle it. How dare she? She paid for her folly, because I held her hand tightly with my front paws and raked it with my hind claws. It was satisfying to see I'd drawn blood. She scolded me, but I simply arched my back, spat at her and after staring at her for a couple of seconds once she had broken free, I simply stalked off in a dignified manner. She learned her lesson. She hasn't done it again.

One day, soon after gaining the living room territory. I had a good look round. I peered into corners, behind furniture and under cushions.

This seemed to amuse her.

"How nosy you are!' She exclaimed.

I am not nosy. I am intelligent and not only interested in my surroundings, but really do need to check everywhere to make sure there is no danger lurking there for an unsuspecting cat. I also needed to be sure that no other feline rival was invading what was fast becoming my own territory. One can't expect mere humans to understand this, or my need to rub my face over everything to put my own personal perfume on it. She calls in slobbering! What a cheek! I have never slobbered in my life.

I knew that I really owned her when one rainy day she found me on her door step looking wet and bedraggled. I put on my pathetic look and she picked me up and towelled me down. Then she let me lie by the fire to get really dry and warm. I had a lovely long snooze for the rest of the morning. When she sat down in her arm chair I jumped onto her lap, laid my head on her shoulder and purred really loudly. She had to admit defeat. She was mine and I was allowed to come and go as I wished from then on. It was so easy!

I don't like to brag, but I have to tell you that I have many skills. I can, for instance, open her back door. I simply jump up, hang on the latch until it clicks open, and push through into the kitchen. Sometimes she turns the key in the lock which means it won't open, so meow loudly until she lets me in. If this doesn't work then I rake my sharp claws down the door and it is very satisfying to see the damage that this does, even though the door is made of very hard wood, it is now decorated with long deep grooves.

I can also open her fridge. Not to steal, you understand, I am not a thief, but I just like to look inside and see what she has in there. It puzzled her at first when she found the fridge door open. Then she saw me do it, but she didn't make too much fuss, she just checked every so often to make sure the door was closed. However, she is inclined to panic when I jump on the sideboard, desk and table where she keeps her telephone. She seems obsessed by the little bits of china and other objects that she leaves scattered about on the furniture, but she needn't worry. I am very careful and haven't broken anything yet.

She also gets annoyed when I have to sharpen my claws on her arm chairs. She yells and claps her hands at me shouting out "No!" in a most unseemly way. She will just have to accept that it is something I have to do. Actually, I think the ragged look suits the armchairs quite well.

The man who lives there with her took longer to accept me than she did, because he isn't here all day, but after a while he was just as easy to win over as she was. Louis, the black cat from next door, told me that I should beware of him, because he was known to hate cats. One day, Louis, the poor fellow was strolling by looking at the bird feeders in their garden, when the man rushed out and yelled and hissed at him, scaring him half to death. Poor old Louis now has to watch really carefully and skirts round the garden in a most wary fashion if he thinks the man is around, although he says he isn't quite as bad these days. Owning this man was a challenge to me, but I soon worked my magic on him, with a little help from her, and one day I knew I had cracked it when I let him hold me on his lap all one snowy morning while he read his paper, and again in the afternoon while he watched a football match on TV. It suited me very well to be in the warm with him, because in spite of my long silky hair, I do come from a warmer clime, and snow is not for me.

Upstairs is a wonderful playground. I can climb in the bath and bat the plug about with my paws. Then given half a chance I get into the cupboard under the wash basin, but she usually grabs me before I get in too far, because I usually send all the little tins, boxes and spare toilet rolls flying, which is fun for me, but seems to upset her a great deal.

I think my most favourite thing though is getting under the bed, where I hide until she comes looking for me, then I grab her feet as she walks by, which makes her laugh. That is a good sign, because then I know she won't tell me off, not that it bothers me if she does, but it is nice not to have to put up with her cross voice.

She spends a lot of time sitting at a machine. She calls this activity 'writing'. One day the machine was chattering away in a most disconcerting way. So I hopped up to have a look at what was going on. I was fascinated by the pieces of paper that kept emerging from the it. I batted a couple, but they still kept coming. This made her smile.

"I have written a story about you." She said. "I am printing it and will give a copy to your people to read."

I watched in fascination at the sheets of paper moving out before my eyes.

"Are you reading it?" She asked with a laugh. "Do you approve?"

Of course I approve. I deserve to have my life with her and her man recorded. I think the main people I own will like it too.

Mind you, everyone of her friends and family knows about me already. She talks about me constantly and tells anyone who will listen about the things I do and how much they both love me. And quite right too.

So that's how I came to add the people next door to my family, and now I have two to attend to. It is hard work, because I have to make sure I spend an equal amount of time with them both. I still have a special loyalty to my original family, because I have owned them since I was a kitten, but these new people need to have my attention too, because I reap great benefits from them. Many other people around know me, because I am rather friendly and very beautiful with my characteristic good looks, but these two families are my main concern.

It is almost a year since I decided to adopt the new people, and as Christmas approaches I realise that with the pleasure of ownership comes responsibility. One has to remember that a human isn't just for Christmas, but all year round.

THE END

Note: I wrote this piece in December 1994. On 5th April 1995, Gwen (Chester's owner) called to tell me that my beloved little visitor had been killed by a car outside our house. I was devastated and absolutely heart broken. He was only two years old and the most beautiful cat I have ever seen. He was a silky long-haired Birman. This piece is my memorial to him and captures his personality perfectly. I will never forget him.

NEW YEAR ULTIMATUM

"Thank you for this evening, darling." Ken kissed Sally over the rim of his wine glass. "It's been a perfect Christmas Eve, hasn't it? But I really do have to go now."

Sally sighed and pulled away from him slightly.

"So when are you going to tell her?" She asked seriously.

"After Christmas, I promise."

" I hope you mean it this time." Sally said sharply. "You have been going to tell her for ages, but you never do."

"I know, " Ken said quietly. "But how could I spoil Christmas for her?"

"What about me?" Sally snapped. "I won't be seeing you at all over the holiday, don't you think you are spoiling it for me?"

"Look," Ken said softly, taking her hand. "Can't you see that it isn't easy. It is going to break her heart that I am leaving anyway and to tell her I wasn't spending Christmas with her would tear her apart. I just can't do it. Goodness knows what she would do."

"I know exactly what she'd do." Sally said coldly. "She'd cry and make such a fuss that you'd feel so guilty that you'd promise her anything just to calm her down."

"She loves me." Ken shook his head. "I know I have to tell and I promise I will, but not until after Christmas."

"OK. When? Boxing Day?'

'She's invited some of her family over then." Ken said sheepishly. 'She's looking forward to it so much. I couldn't bear to spoil her day."

"Fair enough." Sally said resignedly. "But decisions have to be made." She stood up. "I don't want you to think that I am being unreasonable or too hard on you both, but this is my ultimatum, Ken. I want you to tell her no later than New Years Eve. The flat is all ready for us and I want us to move in and be living together by New Years day. It is symbolic, the start of a new year and our life together. If you can't or won't do this, then we are finished. I am fed up with being the other woman in your life. Sick of playing second fiddle to her all the time. You say you love me and want to be with me, then prove it. I love you too, but now is the time for you to choose between us. It is simply a case of her or me. Do you understand, Ken?"

"Of course I do. I know you are right." Ken pulled her into his arms. "I dream of us being together all of the time. I'll tell her as soon as I can after Christmas, and that's a promise."

"Good." Sally kissed him softly on the lips. "I'll be at my parents place over the holiday. Phone me as soon as you have told her. All right?"

"Right," Ken agreed. "We'll be together on New Years day, I promise."

He squeezed her tight. "Thank you for being so patient and understanding, Sal. I know I am weak where she is concerned, but it isn't easy breaking someone's heart."

He straightened his shoulders and smiled. "I'll phone on Christmas Day if I can manage it, just to say hello and tell you how much I love and miss you, and I do love you, darling. Very much."

༄༅

"You're late, dear." said Marie as she kissed his cheek.

"Sorry. The traffic was bad tonight."

"Bound to be on Christmas Eve. People off for the holidays. Glad we don't have to go out anymore for a few days." She said contentedly.

She took his coat and hung it up.

"You're cold, love. Come on and sit by the fire and I'll make you a nice cup of tea, or would you prefer cocoa? Fancy a sandwich.?"

"No thanks, I had something to eat at the pub."

"So that's where you have been." She gave him a slightly disapproving look. "I thought I could smell booze on your breath. Still, I am sure you didn't go over the limit, did you?" She patted his hand. "Put your slippers on, dear. I put them by the fire to warm."

Ken did as he was told and as Marie bustled off to get his cocoa, he thought about his evening with Sally and her ultimatum. It was going to be tough telling Marie that he was moving out.

He had considered just leaving her note, but he knew that was cowardly and cruel. Marie deserved better than that. He had to take the bull by the horns and tell her face to face. She would be devastated at the thought of him leaving, for she was devoted to him. He was her life and he knew he had a lot to be grateful for. He hated the thought of hurting her, but he had made up his mind. It had to be done. His future lay with Sally now, so within the next few days he had to confront Marie. It was time to move on.

Marie brought him his cocoa.

"There you are, dear." she said. "Now we can just relax and enjoy our Christmas together." Her face glowed with happiness. "I've got us a lovely little turkey and all the trimmings, plus the puddings that I made last month. None of that shop bought rubbish." She squeezed his hand. "I can't wait for you to see what I bought you. I know you'll love it. It's going to be a lovely Christmas. Just the two of us. Perfect."

Ken felt even more guilty, but smiled at her over his cup.

೧೦೦೩

The next week crawled by and every day Ken tried to pluck up the courage to tell Marie he was moving out. He managed to phone Sally a couple of times, and each time she asked if he had broken the news to Marie yet.

"Not yet, love. But I will, I promise, just as soon as the time is right."

On the morning of New Years Eve Marie was in a great state of excitement when she got in from shopping.

"I just saw Mary Brown from next door. They are having a big party tonight and have invited us to join them. Isn't that nice? I said I was sure you hadn't made any other plans, so accepted for us both. I hope that is all right, love."

Ken's heart was beating fast.

"This is it!" he thought. "I have to tell her now, or it will be too late."

He cleared his throat and took a deep breath, went over to Marie and took both her hands in his.

"You go to the Brown's party, by all means, but I'm afraid I won't be joining you. You see, there is something I have to tell you, Mum."

Visions of Pompeii
Margaret Faulkner (circa 1983)

The sun-baked city's ancient stones,
Long-hidden secrets now revealed,
Displayed before my wondering eyes,
Time-capsule by volcano sealed.
Ruts worn by a chariot's wheel,
Lanes where Roman sandals trod,
Shrines where supplicants would kneel,
To worship now-forgotten Gods.

Pictures on a noble wall
Painted by a long-dead hand,
Humble pots a servant held,
Filled now with volcanic sand.
The Amphitheatre, still complete,
Where gladiators fought for fame,
No lions now bound across the sand,
No torches lit with dancing flame.

The massive Forum, marble paved,
Still shimmers in the noon-day heat,
And a million tourists tread the way,
That echoed once to Roman feet.
But when the final tourist's gone,
And night-time closes every door,
Does the sleeping city wake,
And come to teeming life once more?

Visions of Pompeii (Continued)

Then, do cool fountains gently play,
In graceful courtyards shady square?
Where the Tragic Poet writes,
And Roman ladies take the air.
Do the Brothers Vetti dine,
In elegant-proportioned room?
Do they break bread with noble guests,
And cups of blood-red wine consume?

Does the dog still guard the house,
Prowling through the peristyle?
A warning of his presence there,
Announced upon mosaic tile?
Do they, within the temple walls,
Celebrate religious feasts?
Are sacred rituals performed,
By Juno and Apollo's priests?

And when at last the morning sun,
Paints the sky with crimson tones,
These ghosts must slowly melt away,
So only lizards haunt the stones.
And so the silent city sleeps,
Still, in the hot Italian day.
Vesuvius, resting, oversees,
The tragic wonder of Pompeii.

CR&O

Eccentric Limerick

A doctor living in Slough
Had a patient with a bad cough
Said the doctor although
My treatment is rough
The post mortem will be very thorough.

SKELETON IN THE CUPBOARD

My beloved Great Aunt Ella was 90 when she died leaving me everything, including the Victorian Villa she had been born in. She had never married, living with her parents until they both died.

When he handed over the keys, the solicitor gave me a letter, with instructions to read it before touching anything.

It read:

Dearest Caroline,

What I am about to tell you will shock you, but please believe me, I had no choice.

When I was fifteen I was seduced by a close family member and became pregnant. My mother realised what had happened and decided that my condition should be kept a secret. As soon as I began to show she made me stay in the house. She told neighbours that I was ill and had gone away to convalesce. When my time came, Mother delivered the baby. It was a boy. She took him away to wash him and when she returned she told me he had died. I was distraught, but she said it was probably for the best, gave me a sleeping draught and told me to rest. When I woke the baby had gone. I asked what she had done with him. Reluctantly she told me that she had wrapped him in newspaper and a blanket and placed him in the little cupboard high above the landing. This was used for storing spare bedding. I protested, but she said we had no option, because we didn't want a scandal. We wouldn't be able to hold our heads up high in the community if the truth came out. We never spoke of it again.

That little bundle is still there. Will you please remove it and give my baby a decent burial. My soul won't rest until it is done.

Please don't be too hard on Mother. She did what she thought was best to protect both me and my father. We were a greatly respected family and the scandal would have ruined us. I am the last in the family line, apart from you, so no one can be hurt now. I have lived with this dreadful secret for many years and feel relieved to have confessed, even if it is after my death.

I believed that my baby died of natural causes, but as I grew older and wiser, I wondered if this was the case, I will never know.

I am so sorry, my dear Caroline, but I can't undo what was done all those years ago.

Please forgive me.

I am and always have been,

Your loving

Great Aunt Ella.

೫೦೦೩

With trepidation, we took the letter and the sad little bundle to the police. No further action was taken and we carried out my aunt's last wishes.

My heart goes out to poor little teenaged Ella and the dreadful things that happened to her all those years ago.

Her story gave more than one meaning to the saying "A skeleton in the cupboard."

POOR
LITTLE COW

"Poor little cow!" thought Ellen as she stood by the bedroom window watching Kelly struggle up the broken path, her thin body bent by the weight of two loaded carrier bags and a worried look on her pinched little face.

Ellen glanced at the clock.

"Six o clock. She's late, she'd better hurry with dinner or she will be in dead trouble".

୨୦୧

Kelly let herself into the house, rushed into the kitchen and dumped her carrier bags on the floor. She lit the oven, took out a packet of oven chips, from the bag, opened it and tipped the contents onto a baking tray and shoved it into the oven. She threw an anxious look at the clock, pushed back her frizzy blonde hair, opened a tin of peas and poured the contents into a saucepan. Then placing a frying pan onto the stove, she lit the gas beneath them both. She grabbed a handful of cutlery from a drawer and set them onto the plastic topped table, where a couple of bottles of sauce and a cruet set were permanently kept. She took a packet of beef burgers from one of the carrier bags, swiftly opened it and placed three in the frying pan. She wiped her hands down the side of her jeans and fumbled once more in the bag of shopping, found a plastic pot containing a synthetic cream dessert, quickly peeled back the foil and tipped the pudding into a dish and set it beside one of the places she'd set. Turning back to the stove, she flipped the burgers, glanced again at the clock, breathed a sigh of relief and the tension left her body.

୨୦୧

Ellen heard Kelly clattering around in the kitchen, and soon the smell of frying burgers drifted up the stairs.

"Thank goodness for that." thought Ellen. "Here comes Frank. She only just made it.."

She looked out of the window as a tall, broad shouldered man of about thirty five strode towards the house.

Ellen's sigh of relief echoed Kelly's.

୨୦୧

When Kelly saw Frank approaching she quickly checked the table, stirred the peas, drained them and took the chips out of the oven.

Frank came into the kitchen.

"Hello, love." Kelly said brightly, standing on tip-toe to give him a welcoming kiss.

Frank scowled. "Dinner ready?" he grunted.

"Just dishing up." the girl replied, putting two plates on the table and dividing the food between them.

Frank slumped into a chair and Kelly sat opposite him.

"Forgotten something?" he growled.

Kelly looked nervously round the table.

"Where's me beer?" he snapped.

"Oh, sorry, love." Kelly leapt to her feet. "I'll get it for you."

Hastily she took a can of beer from the fridge and pulled off the ring. Frank grabbed it from her, took several swigs, wiped his mouth with the back of his hand, belched loudly and continued to shovel food into his mouth.

Kelly picked delicately at her burger and chips, ever watchful, awaiting his next command.

When he had cleared his plate, he pushed it away. Kelly jumped to her feet, grabbed the plate and put it in the sink, then placed the dessert in front of him. He scooped it noisily into his mouth.

"Get me another beer." he demanded.

She got it, took away his empty can and dropped it into the pedal bin.

His meal finished, Frank got up, stretched and yawned.

"Wake me at 'alf past seven." he said, as he lay down on the sofa. "We're goin' to the pub."

"I really ought to do the ironing." Kelly said nervously. "Can't you go on your own?"

"Not likely!" he snapped. "If you think I am leaving you 'ere alone, then you've got another think comin'! There's no tellin' who you'd 'ave round 'ere as soon as me backs turned."

Kelly knew better than to argue, so she piled the dirty dishes in the sink and went upstairs to get ready..

She looked in her wardrobe at the array of cheap, brightly coloured clothes and selected a denim mini skirt and frilly scarlet blouse, with a low neckline.

She went into the bathroom, stripped off and showered, enjoying the cleansing warm water and scented gel. As she towelled herself afterwards she examined her skinny body. Her breasts were small and her hip bones protruded sharply, but she had nice legs and that was what Frank liked about her.

She dried her hair, fluffing and coaxing it into a fashionable style. She applied a little too much make-up to her pretty little child-like face, the innocence of which was betrayed by knowing eyes that had seen too much in her short life.

After spraying herself liberally with cheap scent, Kelly pulled on a black bra and thong, eased herself into the miniscule skirt and red blouse, then giving her hair a final flick, she looked at the clock and rushed down the stairs to wake Frank.

He was snoring loudly, so she shook him gently`. He woke with a start and swore loudly, then yawned and stumbled up the stairs to the bathroom.

He emerged half an hour later, clad in jeans and an open necked shirt. He had had a shave and slicked his hair back with gel. Kelly thought that he wasn't bad looking really, with only a hint of a beer belly, even after all the years of heavy drinking.

He walked over to Kelly, who was perched on the arm of a chair watching a soap opera on TV.

"Come on," he muttered. "Let's go."

Kelly stood up, pushed her feet into a pair of very high heeled shoes and wiggled towards him.

"Come 'ere." he said gruffly.

He grabbed her and crushed her against him, running his hands down her back and over her hips.

"You be'ave yourself tonight, my girl."

"You know I will, Frank." she said meekly. "Don't I always?"

"You better 'ad, that's all." he said threateningly.

෩ඥ

Ellen breathed a sigh of relief as the couple left the house.

"Peace at last!" she sighed. "But not for long!"

She knew that as it was Friday night it would be far from peaceful when the couple got home, for Frank would be aggressive and loud after a night of heavy drinking. It was always the same.

Ellen wandered from room to room, disgusted at the mess the untidy pair had left. Kelly hadn't washed their supper dishes, nor had she cleared away her discarded clothes. Frank's dirty clothing lay in a crumpled heap in the bathroom.

"He always was a slob!" Ellen thought, and wondered aloud why she had put up with him for all those years of heavy drinking, violence and his rough demands on her. Now she had to watch while that poor little cow Kelly went through the same nightmare.

Ellen remembered so well her final night with him. How long ago was it? Two years? No, three.

Ellen had been married to Frank for four turbulent years, when he staggered into the house late after one afternoon, in a foul mood after losing all his dole money in the bookies.

When Ellen dished up his dinner, he moaned that it was dry and threw it at the wall. When she had protested that it was his fault for coming home late, he'd taken her by the shoulders and shaken her until her teeth rattled.

"Don't you argue with me" he snarled. "A man has a right to expect a decent meal after a day's work."

Ellen wanted to say "What work?", but knew she'd regret it if she did, so she meekly cooked him egg and chips and eventually he'd calmed down.

"Get ready." he said later. "We're goin' out."

Ellen selected a modest dress that she felt comfortable wearing, but he'd sneered at her.

"You ain't wearin' that old fashioned stuff." he yelled. "Wear the red dress I bought you."

This was a cheap little number that he'd bought for her in a fit of beery generosity, after a lunchtime drinking session and an unusually successful afternoon in the bookies. Ellen thought it made her look common, because it clashed with her red hair, but Frank liked the low neck and the way the short skirt showed off her shapely legs.

They had gone down to their local pub, where Frank joined his mate Ron at the bar. Ellen was expected to sit at a table with Ron's wife, Pearl. Drinks would appear from time to time, but the men didn't sit with them, although Frank came over to the table once to ask Ellen for money, and she was forced to watch as her housekeeping money disappeared down the throats of Frank, Ron and Pearl, knowing she would have to try and manage on the little she'd kept hidden from Frank for the rest of the week.

A young man at a nearby table smiled at Ellen, and she had quickly looked away.

Pearl noticed and laughed.

"I reckon that fella fancies you, El. He's a bit of all right, don't you think?"

Ellen shrugged. "He's all right, I suppose."

Pearl gave the young man a beaming smile and he came over to their table.

"Can I buy you girls a drink?" he asked.

"No, I'm all right, thank you." Ellen said softly, shooting an anxious look at Frank.

"I'll have a vodka and lime, thanks." Pearl said quickly.

"Come on, let me get you something." he said to Ellen.

"She'll have the same as me." grinned Pearl.

When he went to the bar, Ellen looked worried.

"You shouldn't have done that, Pearl. Frank will kill me if he sees. You know what he's like."

"Don't be daft, El." scoffed Pearl. "It's only a drink."

She hitched up her tight leopard skin print dress another inch and crossed her legs. "Ron will think it's one less drink he'll have to buy me."

The young man came back and placed two drinks on their table.

"There we are, girls," he said with a smile. "I'm Gary and who are you?"

He drew a stool up and sat next to Ellen.

"Pleased to meet you, Gary." Pearl giggled. "I'm Pearl and she's Ellen. Cheers!"

"Can't she talk for herself," asked Gary, smiling warmly at Ellen and placing a hand on her knee.

Suddenly, Gary was jerked off his stool by a furious Frank, who glared at him, pushing his face close to the surprised young man.

"Get away from my missus!" he snarled.

"I'm sorry mate, " stammered Gary. "I didn't know she was your wife, honest."

Frank didn't heed his protests, but drew back his fist and clubbed him to the ground, then began to kick him viciously, yelling obscenities as he did so.

Ellen, her face white with fear, cowed in a corner, unable to do anything except whimper softly.

"Leave him alone, Frank, he ain't done nothing."

Ron pinioned Frank, so he couldn't get at Gary again, and the landlord, yelled at them to get out. With Pearl's help they managed to get him out into the street, although he continued to struggle.

Ellen remembered very little of how they got home, she just recalled Pearl making coffee and Ron trying to calm Frank down.

The next thing she remembered was the two of them being alone in the house, with Frank sprawled on the sofa in a drunken stupor, while she sat at the table chain-smoking and drinking coffee.

Suddenly, Frank was awake, and seeing her he leapt to his feet.

"Bitch!" he yelled. "You two-timing little slag! I'll teach you to mess around with other men."

He lunged across the room and gave her a back-hander across her face.

"Frank, please!" she cried. "I didn't do nothing. I never set eyes on that bloke before."

She cowered against the wall, and felt a trickle of blood running from the corner of her mouth.

"Liar!" he yelled. "I saw how cosy you were. You dress like a whore and then you go and act like one, showing off everything you've got."

He grabbed her arm in a vice-like grip and pushed his face close to hers. She could smell the stale beer and cigarettes on his breath and see the fury in his blood-shot eyes.

She felt his hands round her throat, squeezing tightly as he banged her head against the wall.

"Bitch!" he yelled. "Bloody whore!"

Ellen felt his hands tighten even more until she couldn't breathe, then she slowly sank into oblivion.

ಸಂಡ

How long she had lain there, she didn't know, but the next thing she knew she was sitting up painfully, only to find that everything was quiet. Her head hurt and her throat was sore and dry. Frank was laying half off and half on the sofa. He was snoring loudly.

Ellen stood shakily, then looking down she was surprised to see that she was still lying on the floor, with blood oozing from a wound in her head and dark purple bruises round her neck.

She bent closer and stared. Yes, it was definitely her lying there. She reached out a hand and tentatively touched the blood-matted hair. She drew back her hand in horror. It was transparent! She stood up and looked in the mirror over the mantle piece. Her reflection was there, but she could see right through it. She stared in disbelief and horror.

"I must be dead," she thought. "The bastard has killed me!"

She went over to where Frank lay on the sofa, snoring loudly.

"You rotten bullying pig" she yelled. "You've bloody well murdered me!"

Although Frank didn't hear her, he stirred in his sleep, woke up and looked round the room. Seeing Ellen's body on the floor, he got up, went over to it and nudged it roughly with his toe."Get up, you stupid cow." he snarled.

When she didn't move he bent and touched her cold face. He recoiled in horror.

"Bloody hell!" he murmured. "The silly, bloody cow's dead!"

Ellen watched with some amusement as he panicked. He clumsily tried to revive her, attempted to get her to stand and finally, kicked her in frustration when she didn't respond.

"He's not worried about me," thought Ellen with disgust. "He's only concerned about himself."

She watched with interest when he got a sheet to wrap her corpse in, and she almost enjoyed his discomfort, as he sweated and strained to get her body down to the cellar. All night long he worked, lifting stone slabs, digging a hole big enough to take her body, rolling her into the hole and covering it again, finally replacing the slabs.

"The most work he has done in years." Ellen thought with a wry smile.

Ellen was furious that it looked as if he was literally going to get away with murder.

Yes, the police had called to see him after he had reported her missing, but he told them, as he had told Ron and Pearl, that she had gone off with another man. No one was surprised that she had left him, although Pearl was sceptical at first. After a while no one mentioned her and it was accepted that she had finally found the courage to leave him.

ಬಂಐ

Eventually Ellen quite enjoyed being a ghost as she spent her days wandering unseen around the house. She didn't have to cook or clean for Frank, nor did she have to put up with his drunken fumbling and bullying. She was free of him at last.

She got some pleasure in watching him struggle to look after himself. His pathetic attempts at cooking and cleaning were disastrous, so he lived on fish and chips and other take-aways and the house soon began to look like a tip. He didn't bother to clean out his beer cans and other debris and settled to living in squalor.

After a while he started bringing women home. Just the occasional one night stand at first. Ellen was surprised and not a little disgusted to see that it was Pearl one night. She wasn't bothered or jealous. The only feelings she had for Frank was a desire for revenge. He had to be made to pay for murdering her. She wanted justice, but was content to wait for the right moment, which she knew would come. She just had to be patient.

ಬಂಐ

One night he brought Kelly home with him. A skinny young girl with frizzy hair and broken finger-nails. Her battered suitcase contained a few cheap clothes and down at heel shoes. She was obviously in awe of Frank, and Ellen felt sorry for her at once.

"The poor little cow doesn't know what she's letting herself in for." she thought with compassion.

It was strange watching them make love on her bed. Not that Ellen minded. After all Frank had never been the greatest of lovers at the best of times, and after a night on the beer he was hopeless, but Kelly was young and flattered by the attentions of the older man. She had been desperate to get away from her unhappy home, and Frank was on his best behaviour at first.

It wasn't long before the bullying began. He demanded and got absolute obedience, whether it was for food, sex or household chores. When Frank said "Jump!", then Kelly jumped.

Ellen felt even more pity for the girl.

"I know just what the poor little cow is going through." she often said to herself.

Frank's conscience about Ellen's death didn't seem to trouble him at all. He was as arrogant and demanding as ever, and Ellen was sure that he never gave a single thought for the murdered wife he'd buried in the cellar.

As time went by Ellen watched helplessly as Frank completely dominated the girl, crushing what little spirit she had with both verbal and physical abuse. She was only nineteen and Frank terrified her. He started to beat her about a month after she moved in with him. The attacks usually took place after a heavy drinking session. Ellen knew the brutal pattern only too well.

Kelly often had bruises on her arms and body. A split lip and black eye were badges of her relationship with the hard-drinking older man.

"Why does she stay?" Ellen thought, but then remembered how she had often been asked the same question by family and friends. She didn't know the answer any more than Kelly did, except she supposed that they loved him in a strange way to start with, and then it was fear that held them to him.

Ellen's mother had been abused and beaten by her hard drinking husband and she had no doubt that Kelly's mother was the same. There was often a terrible continuity in these matters.

Once, she remembered, Frank had threatened to throw Kelly out, and the sheer look of terror on the girl's face told Ellen all she wanted to know. Kelly had sunk to her knees and pleaded with him.

"Please Frank," she sobbed. "Don't make me go back there. I couldn't bear it. It was horrible the way my old man used to maul me about when he'd been on the booze. I'd rather kill myself."

"Poor little cow," thought Ellen. "What a life for a kid like that. Having to choose between a drunken father who abuses her or a drunken lover who beats her."

༂༃

The sound of Frank's voice roused Ellen from her reverie. She drifted down to the kitchen and watched in disgust as Kelly helped a very drunk Frank into the house. He could barely stand, but the girl guided him over to the sofa, where he collapsed spilling beer from the can he was clutching over her blouse. He laughed coarsely as she bent over to help him, and grabbed her, pulling her down on top of him, running his hands greedily over her body, as the discarded can spilt its contents over the already stained carpet.

"Come 'ere." he said thickly.

Kelly froze, her body stiff and unyielding, seeing Frank as her father, a scene she had played out too often in her short life.

"No, Frank." she whispered, pulling away from him. "Not now."

"I said come 'ere you frigid little bitch." He snarled, trying to grab her again.

Kelly's eyes were wide with terror, but she shook her head.

"No, Frank, I can't." she whimpered. "Please don't make me."

He lurched from the sofa and caught hold of her skinny arm with one hand, tearing at the red blouse with the other.

"You'll do as you're told." he growled. "You think you can play the high and mighty with me, do you? Well, we'll see about that. I saw you eyeing Ron tonight, you two-timing little bitch!"

Kelly shook with fear and tried to hold the torn blouse together.

"Don't be daft, Frank. I don't fancy Ron, or anyone else, for that matter." she said with a nervous laugh.

"Oh no" he sneered. "You're saying no to me, so there must be someone else." He shook her hard. "Tell me who it is, you slut, or I'll kill you!"

He slapped her hard round the face, sending her reeling, he hauled her to her feet and lifted his hand again.

Ellen could stand no more. She grabbed Kelly, flung her aside and stood in front of Frank.

"Like you killed me?" she asked coolly.

Frank's eyes nearly popped out of his head.

"Ellen! Bloody 'ell, I … I … thought I'd …! "

"Murdered me, Frank? Yes, you did and I am damned if I'll let you do the same to this poor little cow."

Kelly crouched on the floor, terrified, a livid red mark showing on her cheek.

Frank reeled back from Ellen, his face as white as a sheet.

"I've watched you bully this girl the way you bullied me." Ellen said calmly. "But enough is enough. No more, Frank. It's over. Finished."

"Are you going to kill me?" he whined pathetically.

"Oh, how I'd love to, Frank." Ellen said with a grim smile. "But she would get the blame and she doesn't deserve that."

"Who are you talking to, Frank?" Kelly almost screamed.

"Shut up!" Snapped Frank. "Just shut up and let me think."

He suddenly sat back on the sofa, clutching his chest and collapsed in pain.

Kelly rushed over to him."Oh my God, Frank, what's wrong. You look awful."

Ellen, unseen by the girl, whispered in her ear.

"Call an ambulance. Quick."

Kelly obeyed, as if in a trance, though she wasn't aware of Ellen's voice.

༺༻

Frank was taken to hospital. A heart attack was diagnosed and he was installed in the intensive care unit. The doctor told Kelly that he was out of danger, that he was lucky to be alive and praised her for her quick thinking.

"Your quick actions saved his life." he said with a sympathetic smile.

It was well into the early hours when the exhausted girl got back to the house. She fell into bed and slept immediately.

Ellen watched as she slept.

"She's no more than a child," she thought. "Poor little cow deserves better than this."

Just before Kelly woke, Ellen sat on the edge of the bed and whispered in her ear.

"Listen to me, Kelly. When you wake, phone the police and tell them that Frank told you that three years ago he murdered his wife and buried her in the cellar. Do it, Kelly, now."

The girl stirred in her sleep and Ellen retreated.

When she woke, like a zombie, Kelly picked up the telephone and punched out a number.

"Hello, is that the police?" she said. "I want to report a murder."

∞⊗

"Thank goodness for that!" sighed Ellen. "Now at last I can rest in peace. Kelly will be free of Frank, and she can make a new life for herself with someone who'll love and respect her. Best of all, Frank won't be able to bully another woman for a few years at least."

Joyfully, Ellen's spirit rose and floated above the house that had seen so much evil and disappeared never to return.

LOVE STORY

This was a Writers Group Exercise
We had to write in the character of someone of the opposite sex.

I had been stacking shelves at Sainsbury's since my sixteenth birthday, it was boring, but what made going to work each day bearable, was the thought of seeing Melissa.

I would smile shyly at her and she sometimes smiled back. She was beautiful. Even white teeth, full lips, flawless skin and blonde hair scraped back in a pony-tail. Even her uniform couldn't disguise her perfect figure. I was in love.

The only problem was that Melissa was two years older than me, but I was determined that she would see how mature I was. The other lads were always acting silly, pushing each other about and playing childish jokes on people.

I'm not what my school mates call 'cool'. I enjoy English lessons and even write poetry that my family think is brilliant.

I decided to write a poem to attract Melissa's attention, so I shut myself up in my bedroom, took out my pen and began to write. I described the gold of her hair, the beauty of her eyes and the smoothness of her peachy skin. I expressed my love in the most romantic of words. Satisfied with my efforts, I tore the pages from my notebook and put them in an envelope, intending to tape it to her locker.

At work the next day I bumped into Leanne, the mousy-haired girl who hung around with Melissa and her friends.

"Hi!" She said shyly.

"Hi," I replied, then a brilliant idea came to me. I gave her the envelope and said. "Look, will you …."

We were interrupted by the supervisor.

"Work, you two! Now!"

Leanne scuttled off.

Later in the canteen I saw Melissa, Leanne and their friends sitting round the table, drinking coke and reading from a sheet of paper.

With horror I realised that Melissa was reading my poem. She was using a mocking voice and everyone, except Leanne, was giggling.

I wished the floor would swallow me. The object of my dreams was making fun of the words that had poured out of me in such a fervour of love. It was too awful.

The girls rose to leave and as they passed me, they smiled pityingly, except Melissa, whose lovely lips curled back in a n unattractive snarl.

"Poor little kid!" She sneered. "No wonder you can't get a girl friend. You're such a creep."

With a swish of her golden pony tail she was gone.

Leanne slipped into the seat next to me.

"Oh, Joe," She said softly, her eyes moist with tears. "I think your poem is the most beautiful thing I have ever read. And to think you wrote it just for me."

I looked at her sharply, suddenly realising that I hadn't put Melissa's name on the envelope.

Leanne continued. "I really fancy you, but I didn't think you felt the same." She slipped her hand into mine and it felt warm and comforting.

I smiled affectionately. "Fancy going for a pizza tonight?" I said.

FRED
(Written by Molly Holohan-Green in 2005 aged 9)

There once was a dolphin called Fred
Who loved to stand on his head
He blew bubbles galore
And tried not to snore
"Aren't I very clever!" he said.

APRIL
THE FOOL

I was born on All Fools Day, so my parents called me April. Our surname is Pratt. I won't ever forgive them.

I have never been academic, so maybe my name is appropriate.

Luckily, I was pretty, had a good figure, and could sit still for hours, so I became a model at the local art school. A job I enjoyed for several years.

I posed regularly for Cornelius Blackwood, a talented painter. He asked me out and soon we were madly in love. I used a small legacy to buy a rather tatty flat and we moved in together.

Cornelius had no money, so I continued to work at the Art College and earned enough to keep us in food and painting materials.

Cornelius painted me, because it cost him nothing. He was very prolific, and soon every wall was covered with pictures of me in various poses.

I would come home exhausted from work, and pose for an hour or so before I cooked supper. Then while I washed the dishes and cleaned the flat, he would go down to the pub to 'unwind'.

One day I came home to find a note.

"Thanks for everything, April. I couldn't have survived without you, but an artist has to move on. I am going to Paris, where I hope to find success. You can keep the pictures. I can't afford to take them with me. Cornelius."

The bar maid from the Red Lion had gone away as well, I hadn't realised he was seeing someone else. April Pratt by name and by nature!

I wanted to destroy the paintings, but hadn't the heart to, so I packed them away and got on with my life.

Eventually, I met and married Dave Fortune. I sold the flat and we moved into a nice house. Dave was shocked when he saw the pictures, so I agreed to put them away in the attic and that's where they stayed.

Soon after Bella, our daughter, was born, Dave and I were divorced.

It was a struggle on my own, but we managed.

On my birthday last year Bella drew my attention to an obituary in the arts section of one of the broadsheets.

"Look, Mum, " she said. "Didn't you know this Cornelius Blackwood who has just died?"

The article told of his debauched life in Paris, where drink and drugs took their toll and he died in poverty. However, since his death he has been hailed by the critics as a genius, with his paintings fetching huge amounts of money. The writer of the article said that one picture of a young girl entitled 'April', was considered to be a masterpiece. The art world was a-buzz to know if there were more pictures of her.

"Many collectors would pay a fortune for another picture of April." wrote the journalist

"Time to clear out the attic!" I grinned. "I knew changing my name from Pratt to Fortune was a good omen!"

MAY

Sweet May, the pretty milk-maid month,
All blushing pink and white,
Paints the English landscape,
Her brushes charged with light.

She blows softly on the cherry tree,
Until the emerald grass below,
Is littered with its blossoms,
Like drifts of pale pink snow.

With a froth of white cow parsley,
She spreads a lacy counterpane,
Then lights the chestnut candles
To illuminate the lane.

She assembles bright battalions,
A tulip military guard,
To patrol the cottage borders,
And stand sentry in the yard.

MAY (Continued)

She scatters starry blossoms,
On the hedgerows hawthorn boughs,
Then hangs the tall laburnum tree,
With drooping velvet flowers.

She dances through the hayfields
Rich with scented meadow sweet,
And scatters pollen from the buttercups,
Like gold dust on her feet.

She is garlanded with daisy chains
She has lilacs in her hair,
She is warm and sweetly perfumed,
She's the fairest of the fair.

But sweet May, the pretty milkmaid month,
Has come and gone too soon,
So welcome now with open arms
Her rose-clad sister June.

STAND
AND DELIVER

The early autumn sun was sinking quickly, leaving a rosy glow on the horizon. I glanced at the car clock. Six thirty. Time I found a place to spend the night.

The traffic was thinning as I headed north along the A1 … going … ? Somewhere. To be honest I didn't really care. I just needed to get out of London and leave behind the mess my life had become.

A couple of weeks ago Alan and I had just returned from a two week holiday in Crete. I had enjoyed myself, although looking back now I realised that Alan had been a little quiet and pre-occupied at times. I had felt so happy and relaxed in the sunshine, secure in our relationship and our love for each other. The blow when it came hit even harder than I could have expected. I was devastated.

Alan and I first met at my sister Andrea's twenty fifth birthday party. She had invited him along with a group of friends she knew from the gym where she regularly worked out. Alan, at thirty, was a little older than the rest and quite gorgeous!

I am five years older than Andrea, so it was nice to meet up with someone my own age, especially since I was single, having just come out of a long relationship. Alan was also single, so we sort of homed in on each other. We spent the first part of the evening sharing a bottle of wine and chatting and the second dancing wrapped in each other's arms. It wasn't exactly love at first sight, but very nearly!

We started seeing each other regularly and after a couple of months, I moved into his flat. I was there most of the time anyway, so it seemed a logical thing to do.

At first we were unable to leave each other alone. We would come in from work, start to make dinner and end up making love instead.

That was two years ago. Naturally, things cooled down a bit after a while, but I hadn't realised that Alan wasn't as happy and contented as I was. We still made love on Sunday mornings and a couple of times in the week, but looking back now, I can see that the initial passion had diminished somewhat.

The day after we got back from Crete, I was first home from work in the evening, and began to make dinner. My speciality, Spaghetti

Bolognese. I was just sloshing a generous glass of Chianti into the sauce, when I heard Alan come in. I got out two glasses and divided the remaining wine between them.

"Hi gorgeous!" I called. "I'm in the kitchen."

"Hello" Alan replied, without enthusiasm.

He sounded quiet and sort of depressed.

"How was work?" I asked brightly. "Sounds like you have post holiday blues!"

I handed him his glass of wine and kissed him softly on the lips.

"Work was OK," he replied pecking me on the cheek. "How about you?"

"Fine, Not easy to get back into the groove after the great time we had in Crete though"

I playfully cuffed his ear.

"It was your turn to cook tonight, but as I was home early, I'll let you off."

He didn't smile, in fact he looked deadly serious and took my hand in his.

"Forget dinner, Nancy. We have to talk."

"I'm starving," I said. "Can't we talk and eat."

"No." he said with a frown. "Please, Nancy, sit down."

Feeling anxious now and wondering what all this was about, I turned off the gas under the sauce and followed Alan into the living room.

He looked decidedly uncomfortable and couldn't look me in the eye. He took a deep breath and squeezed my hands really tight.

"There is no easy way to say this, Nancy." he said shakily. "But I am asking you to move out of the flat."

"What?" I asked, laughing nervously. "You can't mean it …!"

But he did.

I'll spare the details of everything that was said, but to put it briefly, Alan had been seeing someone he worked with for more than six months. They were in love and were going to get married and needed the flat. Alan's flat.

He was very apologetic, said I had a month to find somewhere else to live and sort out my things, during which time he was going to move in with Alison (his new love) in her bed sit. Then he dropped the biggest bombshell! Alison was pregnant, so it was imperative that she moved into his bigger place as soon as possible, her bed-sit was no place to bring up a baby.

I sat on the sofa clutching my glass of Chianti and froze. I couldn't believe what I was hearing. Soon, I thought, he is going to tell me that it is all a silly joke. He will laugh, take me in his arms and tease me for being so gullible for believing him.

But it wasn't a joke. He was deadly serious. I had been given my marching orders. I had no alternative but to go. It was Alan's flat and if he wanted me out, that was that.

"Why did you go to Crete with me, if you intended dumping me as soon as we returned?" I asked, still unable to grasp what had happened.

"It seemed a shame to deprive you of a holiday you had been looking forward to so much." he said "We ... I thought it would help if you were relaxed when I told you about ..." his voice trailed off and he had the good grace to look embarrassed.

"And does ... Alison ..." I spat out her name. "Know that you made love to me in Crete?"

"I haven't told her as much," he admitted. "But I expect she guessed."

"Oh, she doesn't mind sharing then?" I snapped sarcastically, tears streaming down my cheeks. "Well, I bloody well do!"

I went to hit him, but he caught my hand and held it.

"Please, Nancy," he said desperately. "Let's be civilised about this."

"Civilised!" I screamed. "You're chucking me out so you can have that woman here with you, and you ask me to be civilised?"

I will draw a veil over the rest of what was said. It all got rather nasty and we both said a lot of horrible things.

I packed my belongings during the next few days and left, making sure that everything in the flat was spotless. I wasn't going to have that woman say that I was a bad housekeeper.

I took my stuff to my parents house and asked if I could leave it there until I got settled again.

"You'll always have a home here with us." Mum said softly.

"Thanks, Mum." I said hugging her.

I was grateful, but knew I could never live back home again. I had flown the nest, and wasn't about to return the minute things went wrong for me.

I needed to get away for a while to sort myself out. Laurence, my boss, was very understanding, as he always is, and insisted that I take time off, in spite of having just returned from two weeks away.

"No hurry to come back, Nancy." he said gently. "Take as long as you need."

"Like a life time?" I said bitterly.

"Come on," he said, putting an affectionate arm around my shoulders.

"You'll come bouncing back in no time. You are made of strong stuff."

"Good old Laurence." I thought, as I gave him a watery smile. "Always the optimist."

Now here I was aimlessly driving north, trying to put as many miles as I could between London, Alan, Alison and me.

I had passed plenty of modern motels on the way, but I didn't fancy staying in the rather sterile and impersonal atmosphere that those places offered. I was looking for something with a bit of character. Something interesting to take me out of my dreary thoughts.

Something made me pull off the A1 and drive along an old part of the Old Great North Road and I entered the lovely village of Barnsford. The houses looked glorious in the setting sun. The honey coloured stone buildings almost glowed in the rich amber light.

I spotted the Wheat Sheaf Hotel on the High Street and pulled over to look at it. It was beautiful. The front of the building was original and built from the same golden limestone as the houses around it. I decided that this was where I wanted to stay. Something about the place seemed to call to me.

I followed the signs directing me round the back to the car park and saw that there was a modern extension. This had been built with care and consideration (and a great deal of money!) and it all blended in perfectly with the old part.

I parked and took my case from the boot and walked to the reception area.

The attractive receptionist smiled her professional welcome. Yes, she said, they had vacancies.

"Do you have a room in the old part of the building?" I asked.

She consulted her computer.

"Yes, we have one over-looking the patio and river." she said with another of her dazzling smiles. "It is our nicest room, I think. It has a four poster bed and is the oldest room in the hotel. It is popular with honeymooners."

I didn't really want to know that, and it made me feel even more alone than ever.

"I'll take it." I said.

"How long will you be staying?" she asked, her hand hovering over her computer keys.

"I'm not really sure." I replied. "One night to start with and I may want to extend my stay, if that is all right."

"That's fine." she said reassuringly. "We aren't fully booked, so there shouldn't be a problem if you want to stay longer."

An elderly porter carried my case to the room.

"This is a beautiful hotel." I said conversationally. "Is it very old?"

"The original part is late seventeenth century." he replied. "The modern part was completed about five years ago." He unlocked the door to the room. "It was once an old coaching inn. The stage coaches used to stop here in order to change horses on the journey from London to York."

"Quite a journey in those days." I remarked with a smile.

"Indeed," he agreed. "That's why there are so many of these old inns along the Great North Road." He put down my cases and opened a door to show me the bathroom. "It was a dangerous journey too. Highwaymen often attacked stage coaches in these parts. There were rich pickings to be made, you see, only the rich could afford to travel that way."

"I would love to know what it was like in those days." I said dreamily. "I bet this old building could tell a few tales."

"There are a few books about it in the lounge, if you are interested, and there are several pictures contemporary with the this part of the hotel. They can give you a bit of an idea."

"Thank you." I said. "I will have a look round later."

He pocketed the couple of pound coins I gave him and smiled.

"Thank you, miss, I hope you enjoy your stay here."

After he had gone I had a good look round the room. A canopied four poster bed stood in the middle, and I guessed that it, and the other furniture were either antique, or very good quality reproductions. The soft furnishings were pretty and complimented the period feel of the room. I felt that it had a pleasant and relaxed atmosphere. It had cost a bit more than the other run of the mill rooms, but I felt it was well worth it. I was already feeling less stressed.

I phoned the restaurant and made a reservation for dinner. I realised that I was feeling really hungry, something I hadn't felt since Alan broke the news to me.

I had a long soak in the bath. I had been physically and mentally exhausted, but the scented water and calming effect of the pretty room seemed to soothe away the tension in my body.

Dinner was excellent. Wild duck and locally grown vegetables, followed by apple pie. Everything was perfectly served.

After eating my meal I took my cup of coffee into the lounge and studied the many pictures on the wall. There were a few hunting prints, some water colours of flowers, plus some rather dull landscapes, but those that interested me most showed the inn in its earliest days, plus a few photographs showing the progress of the new extension. Over the fire place was a large oil painting of a lady alighting from a stage coach. She was beautifully dressed in an olive green gown. Her copper-coloured ringlets hung to her shoulders under an elaborate feathered hat. Behind her could be seen the old part of the hotel where my room was situated. The picture showed stables and a yard, clearly recognisable as the patio beneath my window, with the river running behind. There was a label under the picture, but the lighting was too dim to be able to read it properly. The girl looked familiar, so I thought she might be a famous courtesan of the day, or maybe a royal mistress.

By ten o clock I was so tired I went up to my room, took off my make-up and fell into bed exhausted. I fell asleep at once, free from Alan-induced nightmares for the first time in ages.

I don't know how long I had been asleep, when something woke me, although the room seemed still and quiet. A stream of moonlight made a silver path across the bedroom floor to my bed. The curtains were open and I could see the deep blue of the night sky, studded with a million stars through the window.

When my eyes grew accustomed to the gloom beyond the moonlight, I saw a movement by the window. Was it a breeze that stirred the curtain?

Then I saw him. There was a man in my room! I sat up, and my sharp intake of breath made him look in my direction.

I could see a little clearer now and saw that he was tall, had long dark hair tied in a sort of pony-tail with a ribbon at the nape of his neck. His white shirt was frilled at the cuffs and down the front, his breeches were tight fitting, showing off his muscular thighs and buttocks. He wore riding boots.

My first thought was that he must have been to a fancy dress function at the hotel and had accidentally strayed into my room. Maybe I had forgotten to lock the door.

"Who the hell are you?" I demanded loudly.

He placed a finger against his lips and bade me be quiet. Seeing a large pistol lying on the windowsill, I decided I had better obey, at least for now.

"Who are you?" I insisted in a stage whisper. "And what the hell are you doing in my room?"

"Hush, my lady." he said with a frown. "I beg you to remain silent."

"Is this some kind of joke?" I snapped. "How dare you come into my room uninvited and insist on silence."

He peered out of the window and I saw the tension leave his body.

"They have gone now, my lady." he said with a smile, his dark eyes sparkling in the moonlight. "A thousand pardons if I have alarmed you." he moved towards me a little way, then sank down on one knee.. "I beg my lady's forgiveness."

"Stop all this my lady business!" I exclaimed. "It is very irritating. I suppose you are drunk!"

"Not so, my lady." he said looking hurt. "No wine or ale has passed my lips this night."

"Get out now." I insisted, "Before I telephone security."

"You speak in riddles, my lady." he said softly. "But surely you know that I mean you no harm."

For some reason I believed him, but I was still puzzled.

"Who are you?" I insisted.

He rose to his feet and made a sweeping bow.

"Tom Kingsley at your service, my lady."

"There you go again. If you must call me something, my name is Nancy."

He approached the bed and I saw his face clearly for the first time as he stepped into a pool of moonlight. He was about thirty and ruggedly handsome. His eyes were dark and he had a sensuous mouth. A scar ran from eye to mouth, but this only added to his attractiveness.

He sat on the edge of my bed, and I pulled the covers up higher, remembering that I always slept naked. His look of disappointment at this gesture actually stirred me rather than scared me.

"I had no wish to alarm you just now," he said softly. "And I am forever in your debt for not screaming. You saved my life, my lady."

He kissed my hand.

"Saved you life!" I repeated scornfully, "You are inclined to exaggerate aren't you?" I laughed. "Since when has illegally entering a hotel room been a capital offence? Anyway, I am not the screaming kind and I won't even report you if you leave this instant."

"I cannot, my lady, not just yet. Please be patient. I mean you no harm, I swear."

His dark eyes bored into mine and I felt myself go weak.

He reached out and touched my hair. which was loose and covered my shoulders.

"Such a beautiful colour," he breathed. "Like a glossy chestnut, just out of its shell."

He took my hand and I shivered, not with fear or the cold, but with a strange sensation I had never felt before.

He placed his lips against my shaking hand.

"Do not be haughty, my lady." he whispered, causing my skin to erupt into goose bumps. "For tonight we shall know the joys of love as we have many times in the past."

"You must have mistaken me for someone else," I stammered. "I have never seen you before in my life."

"You tease me, my lady." He kissed my lips. "How could I ever forget such a beauty as you."

I could hardly believe it, but I felt myself responding to his kisses, and before long I was making love to this complete stranger, although everything about him seemed familiar, and what we were doing seemed right. I had never known such excitement and ultimate satisfaction.

I don't know how long we spent in each others arms, but the moonlit path across the floor had moved to the other side of the room when we lay together quietly all passion spent.

"I must go, sweet Nancy." He whispered at last. I stirred and held him close.

"Will I see you again, Tom?" I asked as a deep sadness washed over me.

"I pray our paths will cross again, my love." he whispered close to my ear.

He climbed from my bed and dressed himself again in the strange, but attractive garments that he'd flung off as we made love.

"If good fortune smiles upon us, then we will be together again." he said softly.

He lay a finger against his lips and approached the window.

"All is clear, my lady." he said with a sigh of relief. "They have gone and I can make my escape."

"Now whose talking in riddles!" I laughed. "Escape from what?"

"Why, King George's men, of course!" he answered, as if I should know what he was talking about. "For you know there is a price on my head, and I fear your husband has betrayed me."

Before I could say anything more, he kissed me hard upon the lips and bowed very low.

"You are the fairest of all ladies, my sweet Nancy." he said with a smile. "And your wantonness puts fire in my veins, and if it is possible I will return to enjoy these pleasures again."

He paused briefly at the door, and then he was gone.

I lay still for a moment, lost in wonder at what had passed between Tom and me. Then I heard a horse's hooves clattering below. I ran to the window and looked out to see Tom Kingsley mounted on a large black horse in the stable yard. He looked up at me, plucked a white rose from a nearby bush, kissed it and threw it up to me. I caught it and crushed it to my lips. It's strong sweet perfume filled the room.

"Farewell, Tom Kingsley." I whispered, as I watched him gallop over the stone bridge and out of sight.

When I awoke the next morning, I lay still for a while remembering what had happened the night before.

"It must have been a dream." I sighed. "This beautiful hotel and all its history has really got to me in the weird state of mind I am in now."

But laying on my pillow was a white rose.

At breakfast I asked the waiter if he had heard of someone called Tom Kingsley.

"Of course," he said with a smile. "He was famous around these parts in his day. Or I should say infamous. He was a highwayman. A bit of a one for the ladies, legend has it. There's a book all about him in the lounge. I've never read it, but those that have say it is an interesting tale."

After breakfast I went into the lounge and looked in the book case. I saw a leather bound book that was entitled Highwaymen Of the Great North Road. I took it out and turned the pages. Each chapter dealt with a different notorious highway robber. I saw the familiar tale of Dick Turpin, his horse Black Bess and his famous ride to York. Then I found what I was looking for and settled down to read about Tom Kingsley, whose portrait adorned the opposite page.

Tom was known as the Gentleman Highwayman, for he was always courteous to ladies and not violent to men, provided they gave up their jewels and money without a fuss. For a while he stayed at the Wheat

Sheaf Inn in Barnsford and it was here that he met and fell in love with the beautiful lady of the manor, Lady Nancy Bartram, and she with him. Unfortunately, her husband, Henry Bartram, who was much older than her, discovered the liaison. One day he told Nancy that he had business in London and would be away for a couple of days, knowing that she would take the opportunity to meet with Tom at the Wheat Sheaf. Henry told the Red Coats where they would find him. When they arrived at the inn, Nancy hid Tom in her room, as Henry knew she would. However, he had told the soldiers to lay ambush in the early hours along the road from the inn, knowing that Tom would pass that way once he knew he was safe. He was shot dead just outside the village on October 7th 1681. The chapter ended.

"Tom Kingsley's ghost is supposed to haunt the Wheat Sheaf Inn on the anniversary of his death. It is said he is searching for his beloved Nancy"

I looked closely at the portrait of Tom Kingsley and recognised him as my lover of last night. I was shaking as I put the book back into the bookcase.

"Are you okay, miss?" asked the woman who had come in to clean the room.

"Yes, I'm fine," I replied. "I have just been reading about Tom Kingsley. Do you think he really haunts the hotel?"

"So they say." she said. "It's a romantic story anyway. He was a very good looking man, if his picture is anything to go by."

"Lady Nancy must have been quite a girl!" I said with a grin.

"She was certainly beautiful." the woman said. "Even if she was a bit of a hussy!"

"It's a pity her picture isn't in the book. I'd love to know what she looked like.

"Oh, I thought you knew." The woman looked surprised. "That's her portrait there."

She pointed to the picture of the girl in the green gown.

"I hadn't realised," I said. "I was looking at the picture last night and wondered who she was."

"Yes, that is her ladyship!" The woman smiled shyly. "Do you know what, you look a lot like her, if you don't mind me saying."

"Really!" I laughed. "I thought last night that she looked familiar, but the light wasn't all that good."

I looked closely, and I could see that there was a resemblance.

"Mm," I said. "I see what you mean. How weird!"

I said goodbye to the cleaner and went up to my room. The scent of the rose still filled the air as I packed away my overnight things.

I checked out of the hotel and when the receptionist asked if I would come back again, I said I thought it was very likely, but that now I had to return to London and get back to work .

Once on my way I felt much more optimistic. My despair at losing Alan seemed to have diminished completely. I realised that after what I shared with Tom Kingsley last night, ours had been a really half hearted affair, even before familiarity set in. I decided that Alison could have Alan with my blessing.

I made up my mind to look for a flat of my own, enjoy some of the things I had been unable to do because of my commitment to Alan, and generally please myself for once. I was looking forward to independence at last.

Laurence was pleased to see me back sooner than expected, looking relaxed and happy.

He put his arm round me and kissed my cheek warmly.

"You're looking a lot better, Nancy." he said. "The break must have done you good. Did you get yourself sorted out?"

"Of course," I said with a grin. "Just like you said I would."

He kissed me again, and I felt a little tingle. I have known for sometime that Laurence wanted me to be more than a friend and colleague. He is a nice man, and I do find him very attractive, but I need time and a little space before I commit myself to anything romantic again. Who knows what might happen after a while

There is only one thing certain, and that is my intention to return to the Wheat Sheaf Hotel on 7th October next year, where I have a date with an old friend in a bedroom with a four poster bed.

WOOD SMOKE

The late March sunshine warmed Harriet's back as she walked up the narrow lane that led to the wood. A path she had trodden many times when she was a little girl.

Tomorrow was Mothering Sunday, and she had decided to surprise her Mother with a posy of wild violets and primroses like those she had given her when she was a child.

The lane narrowed even more and became a rutted track that disappeared in amongst the trees. Here the path became mossy and soft, deadening her footsteps as she entered.

All she could hear was the sound of bird-song. The liquid trilling of a blackbird and thrush, the incessant name-calling of a distant cuckoo and the chirruping of a dozen woodland species she couldn't identify, under laid with the raucous cawing of the rooks as they busied themselves renovating their untidy nests high in the tree tops.

"I really love this time of year," Harriet thought to herself, and her heart sang with the joy at the sound of the birds and the scents of the springtime wood.

However, something seemed to be missing. Where were all the drifts of delicate wood anemones that she remembered from her childhood days? Where were the clumps of pale primroses? She couldn't see any.

She walked deeper into the wood, heading for the place she knew had been carpeted with swathes of purple and white violets, but there were none.

A movement caught her eye, and looking up she saw an old woman in the distance. She was gathering sticks. Harriet waved to her, but she disappeared behind a tree.

Harriet continued to look for the flowers she was determined to take for her Mother. She searched between the trees and fallen branches, hoping to find what she was looking for.

She had almost given up when she spotted a clump of pale primroses nestling in the root of a silver birch tree. She smiled to herself. Her patience had been rewarded.

Then she saw the old woman again, closer this time. She was bending stiffly to pick up sticks, which she placed in a large wicker basket that she carried over her arm. Harriet blinked and she was gone again.

She knelt on the soft grass, stretched out her hand and picked one of the fragile blooms. She closed her eyes and breathed in its sweet perfume. All the scents of springtime seemed to encapsulated in that tiny flower.

Suddenly, the sweet smell of the primrose was swamped by the acrid smell of wood smoke.

A rough voice croaked in her ear.

"Pretty flowers, ain't they?"

Startled Harriet opened her eyes to see the old woman standing by her side. She was amazed at how quickly someone as ancient must have moved in order to get where she stood now. A shawl covered the old woman's head, almost obscuring the wrinkled face. She wore a voluminous black skirt, that was covered by a grubby once-white apron tied around her middle. Her basket was full of the sticks she had been gathering.

"Yes," Harriet replied. "They are very beautiful, but there used to be so many here when I was a child, now there are hardly any."

"Too many folks do pick 'em, that's why." the old woman said gruffly. Then pointing a blackened finger at Harriet, she demanded menacingly. "Why do 'ee pick my flowers?"

Taken aback by her aggressive tone, Harriet shrugged feebly, not knowing how to answer.

"I don't want 'ee to pick my flowers and plants, you hear?" the old woman continued fiercely. "You must go now. Leave my wood at once."

"Your flowers? Your woods?" Harriet laughed incredulously. "Surely not. These woods don't belong to you, do they?"

"I look after it and all the plants." she muttered. "If I don't there won't be anything left. Not for me or for others to see."

The wood smoke smell grew stronger as she leant closer to Harriet.

"Go!" she hissed angrily, and her bony finger shook with rage as she indicated the path out of the wood, stabbing the air fiercely as she repeated. "Go now, I command you."

Harriet stood up. Her presence was obviously upsetting the poor old soul, and since she had given up any hope of finding more flowers, she decided to do what the old woman wanted and leave. The poor old thing was obviously senile.

A chill wind had picked up, and Harriet was eager to get out into the sunshine again, besides which the wood smoke smell of the old woman was becoming so unbearable that she felt it would suffocate her.

She bade the old woman good bye and hurried out of the wood.

The next day Harriet took her mother the usual Mothering Day gift of chocolates and a bunch of daffodils from the florist. Not what she had hoped to do, but the next best thing.

As they were drinking tea together Harriet told her Mother of her desire to give her a posy of wild flowers picked from the wood in the village, as she had done when she was a child. Her Mother's eyes grow misty at the memories.

Harriet explained how disappointed she was at the lack of flowers in the wood.

"All to do with insecticides and weed-killers." her Mother said sadly. "Selfish people dig up the plants for their gardens too. No wonder there aren't any flowers left. In fact, the Women's Institute has been doing a project on that wood and its history. It has been very interesting, Fascinating actually, because it is quite ancient."

"Then perhaps you know about the old woman who says she lives there." She told her Mother about her encounter and the way she had ordered her out of *her* wood.

The older woman listened intently to her daughter's story.

"Do you know about her?" Harriet asked when she had finished.

"I've heard of her." her Mother said quietly. "She's been seen in the woods a lot lately" She paused, then continued, "I suppose she has as much right as anyone to call the wood hers, and yes, she does live there."

"Does she? I don't remember seeing her before. Has she lived there long? Do you know her name?"

"No, not really, everyone calls her the Stick Woman, because she seems to spend all her time gathering sticks."

"That's right." agreed Harriet. "That's exactly what she was doing. Where does she live?"

"In that tumble down old cottage in the centre of the wood."

"Really? But it is just an old ruin. It isn't habitable surely."

"Well, it's her home. She's a herbalist, though some folk have called her a Wise Woman. She picks wild plants and berries to make her cures and potions. That's why she needs so many sticks. She has a big fire going under her pots where she boils up her potions."

"So that's why she smells of wood smoke." Harriet said, with a smile. "It was so strong that I almost choked."

"It could be that, I suppose." her Mother said quietly. "But it is more likely to be because she was burned at the stake for practicing witch-craft two hundred years ago."

THE SUNLIT MORNING
(Written by Molly Holohan-Green in 2005 aged 9)

Give me the sunlit morning,
Above us in the blue sky,
The birds fly and sing all summer round,
Children play in the sand,
Sea comes up to their ankles,
Summer has begun
Summer time barbecues
Come right round the bend,
But then the leaves start to change
Yellow, brown and red,
Autumn has arrived.

March

Willows toss their long blonde locks
In the brisk, chill winds of March
White clouds hang in the pale blue sky
Freshly washed and starched

Daffodils in serried ranks
Their brassy trumpets raise
To herald in reluctant spring
With a fanfare in its praise

A shaft of sunlight, wintry pale
With warmth that yet deceives
Its fingers probe the stirring life
In new, emerging leaves.

Capricious March, inconstant nymph,
For a moment warm and sane
Suddenly imprisons hope
With bars of icy rain.

Mad month of many changes
Giving hope you can't fulfil,
Stand aside and usher in,
Sweet green, serene April.

BEWITCHED

Dave and Billy pushed aside the bushes that crowded the little cottage garden and walked up to the front door and knocked.

"She's in," Billy whispered. "When she comes to the door, you tell her that we are from the water-board, keep her talking, and I'll look around for anything of value we can nick."

He knocked again.

"Come on you silly old bat!" he grumbled. "She must be as deaf as a post."

"They say she's loaded and has antiques and stuff all over the place."

"My dad reckons she's a witch," Dave sniggered. "She's ugly enough, that's for sure!"

"Maybe she'll let us have a ride on her broomstick." They both giggled.

Eventually, they heard the old lady undoing the locks and bolts on her door, she opened it and peered out at them.

"Afternoon, Madam." Billy said politely. "We're from the Water Board, Checking for leaks."

She looked worried.

"Oh dear, I haven't noticed anything."

"Better be safe than sorry," Billy said. "We'll just come in and check."

He pushed his way past her and looked round the tiny, untidy room.

"I'll take down a few particulars while my mate here looks around for leaks." Dave said and leading her into the kitchen he began to ask her some questions.

"I don't know ... " the old lady looked confused

Billy crept upstairs, entered a bedroom and looked around. He saw a jewellery box on a dressing table, opened it and filled his pocket with an assortment of gold and silver necklaces and bracelets. He grabbed a strange shaped old bottle, a bell with a peculiar design and a couple of ancient candle sticks.

"These look like antiques," he muttered, satisfied with what he had found.

Suddenly, a large black cat that had been sleeping on the bed leapt up, arched its back and yowling as if it had been scolded, ran down the stairs to its owner, where it wound itself around her legs.

"What is it, my beauty?" she asked, scooping the cat into her arms. "Did that bad boy hurt you?"

She looked angry and turned on Billy.

"What did you do to him?" she demanded, her voice shaking with rage.

"I never touched yer rotten old cat!" he yelled.

"Well something has upset him?" she hissed "What are you two up to?"

"Shut up!" yelled Dave. "And give us yer money."

"I don't have any money and even if I had I wouldn't give it to you." the old lady muttered defiantly. "I think it's time we taught you bad boys a lesson, don't you, Midnight?"

The cat leapt from her arms, yowled again and wound even closer round her skinny old legs.

"Huh!" Billy said with bravado. "What do you think you can do to stop us. Gonna set the cat on us?"

They both sniggered.

"Yeah," added Dave, trying to sound braver than he felt. "Reckon you can scare us, you scrawny old bag. We ain't afraid of no one, let alone an silly old woman like you."

The old lady began to wave her hands about, muttering strange words that they didn't understand.

Suddenly, Billy dropped the bag that held the candlesticks, bell and bottle, with a yell.

"The bloody things are red hot!" he cried. "What the Hell is happening?"

The old woman retrieved the things that had fallen from the bag and placed them on the table before her. Midnight, the cat, sat beside them, his strange green eyes glowing with an intensity they had never seen before. Dave took a swipe at it and missed, but it lashed out with razor sharp claws and scratched him.

"I'll kill that bloody cat!" he screamed, dabbing at the blood that seeped from the wound in his arm.

Ignoring him, the old woman continued to mutter, adding a final few words at high volume. The two boys couldn't move, they stood utterly motionless. The old woman stroked Midnight's sleek back.

"What shall we do with these two, puss?" she asked quietly. "We have to show them that they can't go around bullying old ladies and animals. What do you think?"

Midnight purred loudly.

"You ain't gonna do nothing'." Billy said, through clenched teeth. "We are goin' to take this stuff, so get out of the way before we really hurt you and your precious cat!"

"They never learn, do they?" she sighed. "We'll just have to show them."

She picked up the bottle and shook some dust into her hand, then flung it at the boys, as she muttered yet more strange words. There was a great flash of lightening, a roll of thunder, the cottage door blew open and a great gust of wind carried Billy and Dave out of the cottage and away.

The old woman picked up her cat, sat down by the fire and stroked his sleek black fur with affection.

"They won't be troubling us again for a very long time." she said with satisfaction.

Later that day, Dave's mother knocked on the door of Billy's house and enquired if Billy was in.

"No, I'm a bit worried to tell you the truth." Billy's Mum admitted. "He's been gone for ages."

"Dave too, I expect they'll be home when they're hungry. I just hope they haven't got into any more mischief. You know what they're like when they get together."

"Only too well," agreed Billy's Mum.

"You'll let me know if they come here, won't you?" Dave's Mum sounded really worried. "I know they are a couple of tear-aways, but they are still our sons."

"I'll let you know at once if I see them, and you do the same. OK?"

"Of course." she nodded. "I'd better get off home in case they go there first."

Dave's Mum turned to leave.

"Ugh!" she said to her friend. "Mind you don't tread on that horrible toad. It's been squatting on the door step for ages. I keep sweeping it away, but it comes back every time. Nasty, ugly thing."

"That's funny!" Dave's Mum exclaimed. "There must be a plague of them, because I've got one on my doorstep too. It seems to be injured, It has a nasty scratch on one of its front legs."

The two women shuddered in unison.

"Yuk!" they said.

Back in her cottage, the old lady dozed contentedly in her chair, happy in the knowledge that those two nasty boys wouldn't be back at least until the spell wore off. Midnight slept comfortably on her lap.

"They'll probably be too scared to come here ever again." she cackled.

She lay back in her chair and sighed contentedly.

"How long before the spell wears off?" she pondered "I must be getting old, Midnight. I can't remember if it is seven days or seven years?"

The Leopard

Spotted leopard, sleek and svelte,
Sinuously weaves,
Through dappled shadows on the veldt,
Beneath acacia leaves.

Spotted leopard, black on gold,
Hooded yellow eye,
In-built killer instinct cold,
To live his prey must die.

Spotted leopard, gold and black,
With now a splash of red,
A hunter's lethal rifle crack,
Leaves the leopard dead.

Spotted leopard's glossy fur,
Adorns the rich and vain,
How much more beautiful you were,
Free, running on the plain.

THE
NEW TENANT

Naturally, Hetty and I were sad when dear old Miss Peebles died, but she had been getting a little forgetful and we had feared that she would have to move to sheltered accommodation if she got any worse, so it was quite a relief really. The thing that really bothered us was who was going to move into her flat. We were always concerned about new tenants.

What we did know was that whoever it was, she would be a respectable single woman of a certain age. Mrs. Bell, the landlady, only ever let to genteel ladies like Hetty and me. She said she couldn't be doing with flighty girls about the place who entertained gentlemen callers at all hours, so we weren't worried, just curious.

Hetty and I had been neighbours for at least five years. I was here first, having moved in shortly after mother died, leaving all her money to Harold, my widowed brother, who promptly married a most unsuitable bar maid with expensive tastes. Not surprisingly, Harold died of a heart attack soon afterwards, leaving his son Michael penniless.

Mother left me the house where I had looked after her until she died, but I couldn't afford to live in it, so I sold it and was pleased to find this ground floor flat. The rent is reasonable and I live very frugally, so at least I won't be destitute in old age.

Hetty moved in upstairs, next door to Miss Peebles, about six months after me. Mrs. Bell lives across the hall from me, so she can keep her beady eyes on all the comings and goings.

Hetty and I got along well from the start. We were of an age and our situations had been very similar, except it was her father she had been looking after. It was the usual story, single daughter expected to sacrifice everything for an aging parent. Not that Hetty and I complained, well, not much anyway.

My one indulgence is Michael, my nephew. He's a good boy, if a little wild at times and inclined to rash spending. I have occasionally settled bills for him when he has reluctantly admitted to me that he is financial difficulties. No matter, it is a small price to pay for his company. He is the only member of my family left now, and I do feel that he was badly treated by Harold, whose awful wife has long since spent all the money he left her. Michael and I aren't bitter … well, maybe a little, so we comfort each other.

I invited Hetty down for coffee on the morning the new tenant moved in. We had a better view from my flat, so took our cups and sat looking out of the window. Not that we were being nosy mind, just interested to see what our new neighbour would look like.

It was pouring with rain when the removal van arrived and all we could see was a slight figure, swathed in a hooded raincoat, carrying a few cardboard boxes into the house. It was very frustrating.

A couple of days later Hetty came banging on my door. When I let her in she could hardly contain herself. She was obviously excited to tell me something, but I made her wait until I had made us a cup of coffee, before I let her tell me her news.

"Oh Vi," she said at last, her eyes shining with excitement. "I have just been speaking to the new tenant."

She paused to see the effect this news would have on me.

"Viola." I corrected her tartly (I hate her calling me Vi), then added "So what is she like then?"

"Young!" Hetty exclaimed with a snort. "I mean very young. No more than thirty, but a plain little thing. Her name is Julia Morton and she works in a bank in the city."

"Why didn't you ask her to join us for a coffee?" I asked, as I passed Hetty the strong brew, annoyed that she had let the opportunity to meet her slip by. "It would have been neighbourly don't you think?"

"As a matter of fact, I did, but she said she was going to the shops. She asked me which supermarket I could recommend." Hetty looked smug. "I told her we usually go to Waitrose. She thanked me and seemed very friendly."

"What does she look like?" I asked. "Apart from being plain, I mean."

"Very small, only about five two, I would think, with red hair, scraped back in a bun, pinched white little face, no make-up. I can see why Mrs. B let the flat to her. She may be young, but she looks ... how can I put this kindly? ... Uninteresting. Can't see her holding wild parties and having gentlemen callers!" She sniggered. "No, she won't be bringing a lot of excitement into our lives, my dear."

"How disappointing." I smiled. "Still, that's what we want at our age, don't we? A nice quiet life."

It was all a bit of an anti-climax really. We hardly knew that Julia existed. We would occasionally bump into her in the hall, and she would always pass the time of day with us pleasantly enough, but she never accepted our offers of morning coffee, or afternoon tea, but seemed to be for ever in a rush to go to or from her flat.

Hetty was right when she said she was plain. Her clothes were old fashioned and dowdy for one so young. Cheap looking, but certainly not cheerful. She had a penchant for navy, beige or dark brown cardigans and skirts over plain white blouses.

For Hetty and me she was an endless topic of conversation. She intrigued us because she was so enigmatic. It was frustrating that we knew nothing about her at all, except that she worked in a bank.

We asked her to join us on one of our theatre excursions. It was one of the bright new musicals, so we thought it would appeal to someone her age, but she still politely declined our invitation.

Life soon settled down into a rut again and Hetty and I carried on with our routine lives. Coffee together a couple of times a week, shopping on Saturdays and an occasional trip to the theatre or cinema. I watched television most evenings, then read my library book before I went to sleep.

All very boring really, but for Julia, it must have been even duller, because she seldom, if ever, went out at night. She spent all her spare time in her flat and never once invited Hetty or me in for as much as a cup of coffee, although we frequently asked her to join us. Once I asked her to join us for Hetty's birthday supper, but she declined.

Then something happened out of the blue, that gave Hetty and me more excitement than we could ever have anticipated in our wildest dreams.

It was about ten o clock on the evening of Bank Holiday Monday. Always a boring day for me, because Michael was away, most of the other tenants, except Hetty and Julia were on holiday and the house was quiet and depressing.

I had just switched off my TV and was about to get ready for bed, when there was a tap at my door. I looked through the security peep-hole and was amazed to see Hetty standing there.

"Open up, Vi." She said in a stage whisper. "I have something to show you."

I let her in, and was about to admonish her for calling me Vi, when she thrust an envelope into my hand.

"Look," she said excitedly. "This was just slipped under my door. Isn't it peculiar?"

I opened the envelope and saw that it was an invitation.

"Please join me for drinks and a late supper this evening at 10.30pm.

Please bring Viola. Regards Julia"

"How very odd!" I mused, examining the invitation. "We must go, naturally."

"Of course." agreed Hetty. "I wouldn't miss it for the world. I am just intrigued. She has been away all week end, I'm sure, so what an odd time to have a supper party."

We hurriedly changed into something suitably dressy and were standing outside Julia's flat at precisely 10,30.

The moment we knocked, the door was flung open and a completely unexpected vision met our astonished eyes.

"Come in, ladies! I am so glad you could join me at such short notice and at such a late hour, but I really wanted you to come."

I could hardly take in a word she was saying, and Hetty stood struck dumb, her mouth agape..

Julia Morton's red hair tumbled round her face in a mass of springy, shiny curls. She had ditched the horrible glasses and her small oval face was exquisitely made up. Her green eyes, never seen properly behind the thick lenses, were sparkling and beautiful. Gone were the dowdy clothes, to be replaced by stylish and expensive looking clothes. She looked stunning.

Seeing our astonishment, she laughed deliciously, as she ushered us into her room.

"Sorry to shock you, ladies." she grinned. "But what you see before you is the real Julia Morton. I have to admit, for reasons that I really can't discuss at the moment, the dowdy little sparrow that you knew, was not the real me. I hope you approve of my metamorphosis."

"I can't believe it!" gulped Hetty "I would never have recognised you."

"Neither would I," I agreed, "But why … ?

Julia ignored my question and led us to her table, which had been laid for three. We enjoyed a delicious supper of smoked salmon, salad and a creamy gateau. Convenience food, but of the highest quality. It was all delicious.

After we had eaten, Julia opened a second bottle of champagne.

"This, my dear ladies, is a special, but rather sad occasion." she said as she poured the wine. "I won't be seeing you again after tonight. Tomorrow I am going away." Seeing our look of disappointment, she added ""I am getting married, you see."

"How lovely" gushed a rather tipsy Hetty. "Whose the lucky man?"

"Congratulations, my dear." I said, giving her a hug. "When do we get to meet your fiancé?"

"Not possible, I'm afraid. He works abroad and I am joining him tomorrow." she smiled warmly at us. "So this simple supper is just a little thank you to you for everything."

"You have nothing to thank us for." I said.

"You have no idea. You have been so kind to me." she said warmly. "You tried to make me feel at home. You invited me to go on your outings and goodness knows how many invitations for coffee I turned down. I wasn't able to accept, but I did appreciate it very much. Now, let's have a toast to us all." She raised her glass and clinked it against ours. "Here's to a happy life."

Hetty and I repeated the toast and we sipped our wine.

"Now, dear Hetty and Viola, I have to ask you to leave. I have to pack, because I am leaving very early in the morning.

We stood a little unsteadily, and Julia hugged us both.

"Good bye, I wish we had been able to be closer friends. One day you will understand." She opened the door and as we left she said softly. "We will meet again one day, I am sure."

As we made our way back to our respective flats, I felt absurdly bereft. It was if we had been given a beautiful sparkling jewel, only to have it snatched away from us again. I was annoyed to feel tears in my eyes.

I didn't sleep much that night. I couldn't get over the strange evening we had spent with a fellow tenant, whose change in appearance had been astounding to say the least. She had changed from a dowdy little mouse into a brilliant butterfly before our very eyes. I would have passed her in the street and never recognised her. It was truly amazing.

I was up at seven, took in the papers and found a fat brown envelope on the mat. Curious, I opened the envelope and was amazed to find it was stuffed with money. There were fifty, ten and five pound notes, tightly packed together. Scrawled on the outside was a message telling me that there was more post in my pigeon hole in the hall. I retrieved the parcel from the post box and found even more money. With trembling hands I tried to count it,. There were several thousand pounds, I was sure. A note fell out from between the bundles of notes.

I picked it up.

"Dear Hetty, " I read. "You deserve this. Spend some and enjoy yourself. No one need ever know. Have a wonderful life. Love from Julia."

I sat down on a stool in the kitchen, my mind in a daze. I tried to make sense of it all, but I couldn't.

There was a hammering at the door.

"It's me Hetty." said a strained voice. "Let me in, Vi."

I opened the door and Hetty, clad in dressing gown and slippers nearly fell in, clutching a similar envelope to mine and a newspaper.

"Did you get one of these?" she gasped, waving her envelope..

I nodded.

"And have you seen the paper?"

I shook my head, so Hetty spread out the newspaper on the table. There on the front page was a picture of Julia. Not the beautiful Julia of last night, but the dreary little mouse we had known before. A banner headline announced

"BANK GIRL GOES MISSING WITH SEVERAL MILLION POUNDS AND CONTENTS OF MANY SAFETY DEPOSIT BOXES.

Shaking with excitement and disbelief we read how Julia had worked at the bank in a position of trust, and with an unknown accomplice had spent the Bank Holiday week end clearing out safety deposit boxes known to hold many millions of pounds in jewellery, cash and other items of great value. She had left the country, leaving no clues to her whereabouts. She seemed to have vanished off the face of the earth.

Hetty and I drank a cup of coffee and counted our money. There was over five hundred thousand each. A fortune. We discussed the situation over and over again. What should we do? Eventually, we decided that since no one would suspect that a fellow tenant we hardly spoke to would give us some of her ill-gotten gains, we should keep it. We wouldn't go mad and have a spending spree, at least not for a while. Our futures were assured. No more would we have to watch every penny. We were rich!

I was still puzzled as to why Julia should be so generous. It was a mystery that bothered me, but Hetty said "Why worry about it, Vi. Let's just enjoy our good fortune."

A few days later when the post arrived, I was delighted to find amongst the bills and junk mail, a letter from Michael.

"Dearest Aunt Vi,

I was in your area recently, but wasn't able to meet up with you as I had business to attend to. I am sorry about that.

I am getting married soon, and apologise for not asking you to the wedding, but I am living abroad, and won't be able to see you for a while. I can't tell you where I am, but as soon as I am settled I will be in touch. Maybe you and Hetty will be able to visit Julia and me one of these days.

I can't thank you enough for all the help you have given me in the past. Without you bailing me out from time to time, there is no telling what would have happened to me. Because Hetty is your best friend, and has also helped me out a few times as well, I want her to share your good fortune. I know I can trust you both to be discreet. Enjoy your windfall

See you soon I hope.

Love from Michael and Julia

PS I suggest you destroy this letter at once, just in case ….!

I was dumbstruck! My adored nephew was marrying the beautiful Julia! It took me a long time to get my head round that, but eventually I was able to accept the situation

So that was that. The police questioned Hetty and me very gently about Julia, the new tenant, but we said we hardly knew her, and Mrs. Bell agreed that the girl had kept herself to herself. The excitement soon died down and we were left alone again.

That all happened a year ago. Hetty and I are now house hunting. Nothing too flash, but something comfortable for our old age. We are off to Rio de Janeiro next week to spend some time with my nephew and his wife. When we get home Mrs. Bell will be looking for two new tenants.

MY MUM
The Childminder
(Written by Molly Holohan-Green in 2005 aged 9)

I, her daughter, smiles with glee,
As Mum goes round triumphantly,
Looking after kids galore,
But I know she loves me more,

Lunchtime comes along at last,
All is calm, the rush is past,
We have a picnic in the park,
Everyone happy as a lark

Sandwiches and home-made cake,
That I watched my Mum bake.

ENCOUNTER

Saturday morning again.

Lorna climbed out of bed, drew back the bedroom curtains and saw a cold drizzle soaking the February garden.

She sighed, pulled on jeans and sweater, wandered into the kitchen and made herself a cup of tea and some toast.

Her mood was as grey as the day and the weekend stretched out before her like a void.

Sighing, she began cleaning her flat. It seemed a pointless chore, for who was going to see the polished wood, the sparkling glass and the spotless carpet? No one but her.

As she worked, the familiar dull ache of loneliness washed over her and she again recalled the circumstances that had brought her to this lonely life.

She was the youngest of three sisters. Jane and Anna had inherited their mother's beauty and intelligence, but Lorna, quiet, shy and rather plain, was more like her father. She felt completely over-shadowed in the presence of her brilliant mother and sisters.

Jane and Anna left university with good degrees and made impressive careers for themselves, that they later combined with happy marriages to equally clever men. Neither had lived at home since going to university.

When their mother died suddenly, Lorna gave up all hope of higher education and a career, because her father, devastated at the loss of his adored wife and completely unable to come to terms with a life without her, sank into a deep depression and lost interest in everything, eventually slipping into senility. Lorna felt it was her duty to stay at home and look after the difficult old man, which she did without complaint, until he too died.

The family house was sold and the money divided equally between the three girls. Lorna's share was just enough to buy her tiny flat and furnish it modestly.

Now almost thirty, and qualified for nothing in particular, she was grateful to find a dull, but reasonably paid job, doing general office duties for a small manufacturing company. She shared an office with Mr. Church, the elderly wages clerk and Mrs. Burton, the formidable matron who was secretary to the Managing Director.

Lorna got along perfectly well with her colleagues, but didn't socialise with them out of working hours. Because of the age difference, apart from work, they didn't have much in common.

When the flat was cleaned to her satisfaction Lorna made a cheese omelette for her lunch. Looking out of the window she saw that the drizzle had stopped and a watery sun was trying to break through the clouds.

She showered, dressed in a warm sweater and skirt, threw on her top coat and decided to go into town to do some window shopping to cheer herself up.

The cold air refreshed her, and as she mingled with the Saturday afternoon crowds, her spirits lifted. She felt less alone.

She wandered round the shops, ending up in the towns only departmental store, where she was tempted to buy a scarlet sweater, the brightness of which cheered her.

Pleased with her purchase, she decided to go up to the cafeteria at the top of the store for a cup of tea and a cake. Anything to delay going home. She was reluctant to return to her lonely flat.

She made her purchases and looked round the crowded cafeteria for a table and saw there was just one unoccupied by the window. She sat down and slowly sipped her tea and nibbled on the cake.

ഩരു

As Jim hauled his carrier bags through the crowded street, he wondered if he would ever get used to having to spend his Saturday afternoons shopping.

Before Shirley left him he had always enjoyed a couple of pints with his mates, before they all went off together to watch their local football team play. Now he had to pay to keep Shirley and the kids in the house, as well as renting a pokey little bed-sit for himself, there wasn't enough money to do those things anymore, nor the time. He worked as much overtime as he could, which included Saturday mornings, so now he had to shop for his groceries in the afternoon, a chore he didn't enjoy.

Cold, tired and depressed, he decided to get a cup of tea and a doughnut, before returning to his lonely room. He made his way to the departmental store, took the escalator up to the cafeteria, made his purchases and looked for a seat. He spotted a table by the window with just one young woman sitting at it. He approached it.

"Do you mind if I sit here?" He asked.

She looked up shyly and shook her head.

"Not at all." she murmured and quickly looked away.

Jim sat down and sipped his tea and as he did so, he surreptitiously looked at the young woman. She looked nice, and even though she wasn't all that pretty, she had a sweet face. About thirty he reckoned and noted that she wasn't wearing any rings.

He would have liked to start a conversation, but ever since Shirley had left him for another man, he had lost confidence. He was out of practice at chatting up women.

ಸಿಂಞ

Lorna had almost finished her tea and cake when the man sat down at her table. She had liked the sound of his voice and noticed that he was tall and quite attractive. She would have loved to get into a conversation with him, just to get some interaction with another human being before returning to the loneliness of her flat. She was too shy to speak first, but would have responded had he spoken to her. Their eyes met for a second and she thought he was going to say something, but he quickly turned away, so she drained her cup and stood up to leave.

ಸಿಂಞ

Jim's heart sank as she rose from her chair, he had missed his opportunity and would never know if she was as nice as she looked.

When Lorna stood and stooped to gather her parcel, her sleeve caught her empty cup and it crashed to the floor, breaking into several pieces.

Flustered, she blushed and said "How clumsy of me!"

"Don't worry," Jim smiled. "I'll pick up the pieces."

As they both stooped to gather the broken shards, their eyes met and their hands touched briefly.

"Sorry," they both said simultaneously and smiled self-consciously. They held their gaze for a moment, then suddenly overcome with shyness, Lorna murmured a quiet "Thank you." and hurried away, leaving Jim alone at the table. He cursed himself softly for not saying something to keep her there.

ಸಿಂಞ

That night, as she ate her solitary meal, Lorna thought about the man in the cafeteria. She blushed, recalling her embarrassment at knocking over the cup. How kind he was. If only they could have exchanged a few words, who knows what it might have led to.

"Stop this nonsense," she told herself sternly. "A man like that would never be interested in a plain little mouse like me,"

ಸಿಂಞ

Jim stared at the ceiling, thinking about the young woman he had seen that afternoon.

"It was fate that she knocked over that cup," he told himself. "I had the perfect opportunity to talk to her, but I was too stupid to take the chance. If only I had a bit more nerve, we might have got talking and could even have spent the evening together."

He banged the arm of his chair in frustration.

"Pure fantasy!" he declared. "I don't know why I should think she would be interested in me. I expect she has a boyfriend already." He sighed. "Still, it would have been nice."

Resignedly, he picked up the carrier bag of shopping, from where he had dumped it and brought out a can of lager. His Saturday night treat. As he removed it from the bag a small white label fluttered to the floor.

He picked it up and saw that it was one of those address labels that charities sometimes give to people who donate to them.

He read the name Miss Lorna Grey, followed by a local address and telephone number.

His spirits rose as he realised that the label must have fallen out of the woman's purse as she tried to pick up the broken china.

He grinned widely, and thanked the fates for giving him another chance. This time he wouldn't let it go, then with a feeling of elation, he reached for the telephone and began to punch out Lorna's number.

THE PROPOSAL

Julie had only ever had one ambition and that was to get married, but by the age of twenty-nine she still hadn't managed to secure the husband she dreamed about.

Over the years she had been out with many eligible young men, but they always faded from the scene before she could get the longed for engagement ring on her finger. Her mother said her keenness to settle down drove them away.

Then she met Darren. He was tall, dark, and though not quite handsome, he did have a flat of his own. He was a perfect gentleman and treated her with kindness and consideration. Although he wasn't exactly as passionate as she would have liked, he was very affectionate.

They had been dating for about six months when Julie snuggled up to him one night and told him that she was sure that this was the real thing, the love she had dreamed about. She was a little disappointed when he didn't return her declaration of love, but was reassured by his warm kisses.

As much as she loved him, she told her mother firmly that she wouldn't live with him. Not that he had asked her to (although her mother didn't know that), but she was sure that it was just that he had too much respect for her to ask her to live in sin. He wanted to save all that side of things until they were married. He really was a gentleman with old fashioned values, she thought.

Julie set about making herself indispensable to him. At weekends she would clean his flat, shop for food and cook delicious meals to put in the freezer to see him through the week. She even did his washing and ironing. Every Saturday he went out to watch his football team play, and when he got back Julie was dressed in her most seductive clothes, had supper on the table, with a bottle of wine opened. He really appreciated all she did for him and told her so. Julie glowed from his compliments.

"He must see what a good wife I would make," she thought, as she folded his immaculately laundered shirts, or vacuumed the flat. "I just have to be patient."

Then Darren started to work late at the office. Julie didn't mind, because this gave her the opportunity to go round to the flat and cook for him in the week. He was always grateful and occasionally bought her flowers to thank her.

One Saturday morning she had just popped into the supermarket to buy the ingredients for Darren's supper when she saw him on the opposite side of the road. She was about to call out to him, when she saw him go into the little jeweller's shop where she had often admired the engagement rings.

Her heart leapt as she pictured him choosing one for her.

She hurried home, full of excitement and told her mother what she had seen.

"Don't build your hope up too much, love" warned her mother. "You know how disappointed you've been in the past."

"Oh Mum, can't you see," Julie sighed. "It all makes sense. That's why he's been working over-time. He's been saving for a ring for me."

She extended her hand and gazed at it.

"Will he choose diamonds or rubies? Maybe a sapphire. One stone or three?"

She grabbed her mother and swung her round the kitchen in a wild little dance.

"Isn't it exciting? At last, I will be a bride!" she giggled happily. "I just know that I am right!"

"I hope so," her mother murmured.

Julie's phone rang. It was Darren.

"Hi, Julie!" His voice gave her goose bumps. "Look, don't cook dinner for me tonight. I want to take you to Angelo's for dinner. I have something important to say to you. I'll pick you up at eight."

When he'd gone Julie was bubbling over with excitement.

"See, Mum!" she said, her voice shaking with emotion. "I told you so. He's taking me to the most expensive Italian restaurant in town and he's going to propose. Your little girl is going to be a bride before this year is out!"

"I hope you're right, love." said her mother with the resignation of one who had heard it all before.

Julie spent the afternoon getting ready for her special date. She had her hair done, wore her prettiest dress and dainty shoes. She even lashed out on a manicure at the nail bar. Her hands had to look perfect for the moment he slipped the ring on her finger. This was it! She had cracked it at last!

The restaurant was crowded, but they were shown to their reserved table in a secluded corner. The waiter smiled in open admiration as he drew out her chair for her. She knew she looked good and smiled back at him.

There were fresh flowers on the table, the cloth and napkins were snowy white. Everything was perfect in fact. A perfect setting for a romantic meal.

Julie wondered if he would propose discreetly, or drop down on one knee, so that all the other diners would be envious of her romantic moment of triumph. She was shaking a little with excitement and anticipation.

The waiter was efficient, the wine was excellent and the food delicious, although Julie was aware that Darren seemed a little ill at ease and distracted while they ate. He didn't even notice when the waiter brushed Julie's hand occasionally and seemed to be over attentive to her. She hoped he might get a little jealous.

"Still" she thought. "I expect he's nervous, after all it isn't every day that a man proposes to a girl."

After draining his glass and picking at his dessert, Darren leaned across the table and took Julie's hand in his, and smiled a little shyly at her.

"Julie," he said quietly. "There's something I have been wanting to say for ages, but …" he sighed and shook his.

"I think I know what you are going to say." Julie said with a warm smile.

"You do?" Darren looked surprised. "I had no idea that you'd guessed. Still I suppose you can't expect to keep things quiet in a small town like this."

Seeing Julie's puzzled look, he squeezed her hand a little harder.

"Since you seem to know what this is about, I had better tell you the whole story." He smiled sweetly at her. "I have always known that I was different, and although I was very fond of you and loved you like a sister, something was missing, but I didn't know what it was until I met Justin …."

"Like a sister? Justin?" Julie couldn't believe her ears. "Who the hell is Justin?"

"That gorgeous blonde guy who works in the jewellers in the High Street. I've been seeing him for a few months now. I am sorry, I lied when I said I was working. I would have told you before had I known you were going to be so understanding about it. He's moving in with me next week."

Julie's face turned red and her eyes filled with tears and Darren looked embarrassed.

"I'm so sorry. I didn't mean to hurt you. You're very welcome to come and visit us …"

Julie was incandescent with rage.

"You heartless beast!" she hissed. "Why humiliate me by bringing me here and dumping me in public?"

"That's not what I wanted to do. I just wanted to thank you for being such a wonderful friend to me."

"Friend?" Julie said through gritted teeth. "I can't believe that you could be so insensitive. Get out! Go on, leave me … now! Go to your precious Justin. I hope he can cook as well as me!"

Darren looked a little sheepish, but also relieved. He got up, kissed her briefly on the cheek, whispered a brief "Good-bye and thank you." and left.

Julie just sat at the table, too stunned to move, wondering how in a few minutes her whole world could have come tumbling down round her ears.

A quiet voice spoke to her. It was the waiter.

"Sir has paid the bill," he said, then looking concerned he added. "Is Madam all right?"

"I've had a bit of a shock." said Julie, dabbing at her eyes. "Will you call me a taxi?"

"Certainly, madam," he said. "However, I am going off duty in a minute and if madam would permit, I would be very happy to run you home."

Julie looked up at him and through her tears and noted that he was good looking and wasn't wearing a wedding ring. She thought that he must be doing all right if he owned a car. She dabbed at her eyes again and smiled wanly up at him.

"That would be very kind. Thank you." she murmured.

She was beginning to feel better already

MOLLY'S CHRISTMAS POEM
(Written by Molly Holohan-Green in 2005 aged 9)

The people of Godmanchester town,
Went out to sing carols
As the cold snow fell down
They had scarves and hats,
Gloves coats as well,
It was as if a curse was on them,
Making an icy spell.
The path was frozen
And slippery under foot,
The someone arrived,
Who was covered in soot.
It was Father Christmas,
With a bag full of presents,
Then Dad returned,
With the Christmas pheasants.

SUMMONS
(Written by Molly Holohan-Green in 2005 aged 9)

Out of the darkness
I call to thee
To step forward
Come to me

THE LOVING NIECE

Jane slid the letter she was writing to Alex into the drawer, and pulled the one she had just written to her aunt towards her, as Derek entered the room.

"Did you get him?" she snapped.

"Yes dear. He's in a basket in the garage." her husband replied meekly.

Jane shuddered.

"I can't bear to think of that smelly old cat being anywhere near me, but I suppose the garage is better than the house." she said "Still, I suppose it will be worth it in the long run."

"Shall I butter his paws?" Derek asked quietly.

"Butter what you like." snapped Jane. "Just keep the filthy creature out of my sight, but be sure to keep him safe, he could be worth his weight in gold."

She picked up the letter from her desk and passed it to Derek.

"Here," she said. "See what I have written."

He took the letter and read aloud.

"My dearest Aunt Norah,

We were so sorry to hear of your latest heart attack, and we both wish you a speedy recovery. Please don't worry about Tiddles. Your dear old pussy-cat will be well looked after here until you return home. Derek has collected him from your house, and checked everywhere to make sure that all is safe, sound and secure. Tiddles seems to be settling down with us, although I am sure he is missing you.

We insist that you come to us to convalesce when you get out of hospital. You know that we will love having you here as always, and you must stay as long as you like. Now just you concentrate on getting well again and don't worry about a thing. We both love you very much. God bless.

Your loving niece
Jane xxx"

"That's very nice, dear." Derek said with a tear in his eye. "Huh!" said Jane. "Let's hope she soon snuffs it. I can't bear to think of that stinking cat staying here for long." She glared at Derek. "Go on, you had better sort something out for her beloved Tiddles, and don't forget to de-flea the nasty smelly creature."

"Very well, dear." Derek trotted off obediently to do her bidding.

"Wimp!" Jane hissed under her breath, taking out the letter she had hidden in the drawer.

"Now where was I?"

She read what she had already written.

"My darling Alex,

I can't tell you how much I have missed you, my love. I can't e-mail as the computer has crashed, but I will phone as soon as an opportunity arises. In the meantime, we must be patient. Aunt Norah has had another heart attack, and isn't expected to recover. Hopefully, this one will be the fatal one I have been praying for. She is over eighty, and as I am her only relative, I expect to inherit everything. She has a huge house stuffed with antiques, where she lives with her disgusting old cat as her only companion. God, when I think of the hours I have spent being nice to the old hag and the appropriately named Tiddles, I could scream! I have really earned my inheritance. I have sucked up to the old fool for years and she has fallen for it. Dopey Derek really does seem to like her, so she loves it when we visit, and is always telling us that everything will go to us when she dies. Well, hopefully, that day isn't far off. I can't wait to dump that spineless wimp of a husband of mine, then you and I can start a new and rich life together the way we have always planned. I'll be in touch when I can. Until then, my angel, I'll be thinking of you all the time. It is frustrating to know that you are so near and yet so far. I love you.

Your adoring Jane."

She added a row of kisses.

Derek came into the room carrying a large tabby cat, so she hurriedly covered up her letter to Alex with the one she had written to Aunt Norah.

"Ugh! Don't bring that hideous creature in here!" she exclaimed wrinkling her nose with disgust.

"I think he's rather sweet." Derek said softly, as he stroked the cat's soft fur. "Listen to him purr."

"Sweet!" exclaimed Jane incredulously. "You'll be saying that Aunt Norah is a nice old lady next."

"As a matter of fact, she is." Derek smiled. "I really like her."

"Well all I can say is that you are easily pleased."

"She's always nice to me." Derek said defensively.

"Of course she is." snapped Jane. "You dig her garden for her, and run around after her all the time, don't you?"

"She's old and frail and is always so grateful for everything. I enjoy doing things for her."

"Oh for goodness sake." Jane said impatiently. "Just get that cat out of my sight. I am off to post this letter, I want it to get there in the morning, hopefully before she pops off." She gave a harsh and humourless laugh.

"At least she'll die happy then, knowing how much her niece loves her!"

"Really, Jane." Derek said looking shocked. "You can be so hard at times. "I hope she gets better quickly. I will enjoy her staying here. She is such good company."

"I sincerely hope it won't come to that. The last thing I want is a smelly old lady and her equally smelly old cat hanging around the house all day and getting in the way."

When Derek left the room, Jane popped the two letters into envelopes, addressed them and hurried down the road to catch the last post.

"Good" she said, "They will get there in the morning."

Derek spent the evening making a cat flap for the garage door, and arranging Tiddles basket in a cosy corner out of the draught. Meanwhile Jane sat at her desk making calculations and planning her new and exciting life with Alex, away from the boring wimp of a husband when she inherited Aunt Norah's wealth. She was so excited at the prospect, she could hardly breathe.

"Soon," she whispered. "Let it be soon."

The hospital phoned early the next morning. The nurse told Jane that Aunt Norah was a lot better. Her heart sank when she was told that the old lady had told the doctors that she was going to convalesce at her niece's home, where she would be well looked after. The doctor's agreed that she would be much better at home with a devoted relative, than in hospital, so they had arranged for her to be discharged later that day and looked forward to seeing them when they collected her.

Jane cursed after she'd hung up.

"Damn! The old bat's recovered yet again!" she said angrily. "She must be tough as old boots."

"That's wonderful news." Derek said genuinely pleased. "I'll go and fetch her now. It is quite a journey there and back and I don't want to keep her waiting."

He sang softly to himself and he prepared to leave Jane for the journey. It really would be nice to have the old lady with them for a while. She had a great sense of humour and they always enjoyed doing the Times crossword together every day.

As soon as Derek was on his way, Jane phoned Alex.

"It's not good news, darling," she said. "The old girl has recovered. Derek has gone to collect her, and will be gone a good three hours, so why don't you come over now. We won't be able to meet up for a week or two now, which is really frustrating, so let's make the most of this opportunity."

Within half an hour Alex and Jane were in each other's arms, entwined in passion on the bed that was to be Aunt Nora's during her convalescence.

They were lying back enjoying a glass of wine when Jane noticed the time.

"You had better go, darling." she said. "They will be home soon. I could explain your presence to daft Derek, he would believe anything I told him, but the old girl is as bright as a button and would be suspicious."

Alex got up and pulled his clothes on reluctantly. Jane pulled him to the door and kissed him goodbye. As he felt in his pocket for his car keys, he smiled broadly.

"Ah yes," I meant to tell you about this." he said with a laugh.

He handed her a crumpled letter.

"A Freudian slip, I think, sweetheart! You addressed your Aunt's letter to me. Better have it back and put the right address on it, if it isn't too late."

Jane blanched and snatched the letter from his hand.

"Dearest Aunt Norah ..." she read.

"Oh my God!" she cried. "Then she must have got the one meant for you ..."

Just then they heard a car door slam. Looking out of the window Jane saw Derek helping a grim-looking Aunt Norah out of the car.

Then as they heard Derek's key in the lock, a worried looking Jane grabbed Alex's arm.

"What are we going to do?" she squealed. "Quick, think of something!"

November

Through the iron railing sifts
Herded by an icy gale
Fallen leaves in golden drifts
Blazing their autumnal trail

The naked shrubs drip endlessly
Our breath hangs in the clouded air
It's almost dark by half past three
And the dismal garden's cold and bare

The watery sun, low in the sky
Has no warmth to melt the frost
The bonfire smoke drifts slowly by
Curls like a cloud and then is lost

November (Continued)

Withered apples on the bough
Scarlet hips and crimson haws
Food for birds, so hungry now
These visitors from colder shores.

The skeletons of summer trees
Naked now against the sky
Shiver in the chill, damp breeze
Wrapped in fog as if to die.

This is the bleakest time of all,
The death throes of another year.
The melancholy end of fall.
Yes, November, no, no cheer.

ॐ

TIMMY

Paula closed the book and bent to kiss her daughter.

"Goodnight, sweetheart," she said, gently brushing back the soft dark curls. "Time to go to sleep."She kissed the little girl fondly, and pulled the covers over her.

"Will I see Daddy tomorrow." Emily asked.

Paula felt the familiar over-whelming sadness sweep over her again.

"No, darling," she said softly. "I told you, Daddy has gone to live with the angels in Heaven."

"Why didn't he take us with him?" Emily asked, with tears in her eyes.

"He wasn't allowed to." Paula explained.

Emily lay down again and closed her eyes.

"I see," she said with a sad little sigh.

"Oh, dear," thought Paula. "I'm not making a very good job of this. It's so hard to explain to a four year old about the death of her father."

Thankfully, Emily seemed to accept what she had told her, for without any more questions she snuggled down in her bed.

"Good night, Mummy," she said. "God bless."

"Good night, darling." Paula kissed her daughter again and turned to leave.

"Don't forget to kiss Timmy too," Emily called.

"Whose Timmy?" Paula asked curiously.

"My friend, of course." Emily said indignantly. "See, here he is."

Emily patted the pillow beside her.

"Isn't Mummy funny," she said to it. "She doesn't know that you are here."

She chuckled softly and added. " Timmy's my new friend, Mummy. Kiss him goodnight too."

Paula kissed the air above the pillow.

"Goodnight, Timmy." she said with a smile.

୨୦ଓ

Paula joined her parents in the drawing room. Julia, her mother, looked up and smiled.

"Did she settle all right?" she asked.

"Eventually," Paula sighed. "But I had to read her an extra long story tonight. She's acquired a new friend. He's called Timmy." She smiled. "Didn't I have an imaginary friend when I was her age?"

"Yes," Julia laughed. "A naughty little girl called Bluebell as I recall. At least that's who you blamed for any mischief that you got into."

"I suppose it is quite normal for children to have imaginary playmates, isn't it?" mused Paula "But I do worry about Emily. I don't want to become over-protective, but the poor little mite has had so many upheavals in her short life. First Martin's illness, then his death and I hate to think what leaving the only home she has known and all her little friends at play school must be doing to her." Paula's eyes misted over and she bit her lip. "She's a stoical little girl, but it must affect her."

Julia put an arm round her daughter.

"It hasn't been easy for you either," she said. "Thank goodness we had room for you both here ."

"You and Dad have been so good to us," Paula said, hugging her mother. "I don't know how I would have coped without you."

"It's just lucky that we decided to buy this house when we did." Peter looked up from his newspaper.

"Who decided to buy it?" he asked wryly.

"Okay," Julia laughed. "I know, I know. It was my idea, but I just fell in love with the place and you have to admit that you love it too."

"Of course I do, " Peter agreed and turned back to his newspaper.

Julia looked out of the window at the tangled garden, which was bathed in the soft light of the summer evening.

"It will be lovely when it is all sorted out." she said with a smile. "The weather forecast is still good, so while Peter gets on with the garden, I think you and I should sort out the attic, Paula."

"Sounds good to me," she agreed. "I am itching to rummage through all that stuff. There's no telling what we might find up there, From what I can make out it hasn't been touched for years."

"As long as you don't find an old skeleton in a trunk, or some other sinister secret," joked Peter

Paula shuddered at the thought. " Please, Dad, don't even joke about such things," then quickly changed the subject.

"I have put Emily's name down to start at the village school in September. It's a pity that there are no kids her age living nearby to play with her until then. Still, she has this big garden to play in all summer."

"And now she has Timmy to keep her company," laughed Julia.

"Ah yes, I was forgetting about Timmy." said Paula.

ಸಿ‌ಂಡ

At breakfast the next morning, Emily happily ate her cereal, but asked for some toast for Timmy.

"Timmy don't like cornflakes." she said, then turning to the empty chair that she had insisted was placed beside her, added. "Do you, Timmy?"

Paula grinned as Julia took a slice of bread and placed it in the toaster. When it popped up, Emily laughed.

"That made Timmy jump!"

When Julia had buttered it and put on a plate in front of the empty chair at the table, Emily shook her head.

"Timmy says that's not toast." she looked intently at the chair, then back to Julia. "He says you make toast with a fork in front of the fire, not like that."

The two women looked at each other with surprise, but Emily asked permission to get down from the table so that she and Timmy could go out to play.

"Off you go, darling," said Paula, "But don't go out of the gate, will you?"

"Course not." Emily assured her. "Timmy is going to show me the garden."

They watched as the little girl trotted off into the sun-lit garden. What a charming picture she made in her little pink cotton shorts and white T-shirt. Her dark curls bobbing on her shoulders as she laughed and chatted non-stop to her imaginary friend.

"I suppose it's harmless?" Paula said quietly.

"What? Oh, Timmy, you mean?" Julia replied. "Oh yes, it didn't do you any harm. Kids everywhere have imaginary friends. It's quite normal."

"Is it because she's lonely?"

"Maybe, but it is probably connected with losing Martin and her little friends from play-school. She has invented Timmy to compensate and it's a friend no one can take away from her." She put a hand on Paula's arm. "Come on, don't worry, she'll be just fine. She seems happy out there and Peter can keep an eye on her. He's working in the garden." She grinned. "Let's go and see what we can find in the attic."

The two women climbed the ladder up into the attic and were soon absorbed in sorting through the piles of papers, boxes and trunks that had been stored there for generations. They could hear Emily chatting and laughing with Timmy and Peter in the garden, and Paula soon relaxed and began to enjoy the task.

༄༅

As the long summer passed, Timmy became an integral part of the family, accepted by them all as Emily's constant, but invisible companion. However, she always left him at home when they went into the village to shop, or on any other excursions. When Paula asked if he would like to accompany them on a trip, Emily shook her head.

"Timmy don't like motor-cars. He says they are too noisy and he gets frightened."

She would sometimes ask if she could take home a small gift for him and was allowed to do so.

On one of their trips to the village Julia bought Emily a new dress, and as she was trying it on the little girl smiled broadly.

"I like this colour, Granny, 'cos Timmy has blue eyes just like the colour of this dress."

Julia ruffled her granddaughter's dark curls.

"And does he make a fuss when his hair is brushed like a certain little girl I know does?"

"No," Emily said sulkily. "His hair is different to mine. It's yellow and it don't have curls and tangles, so it don't hurt when it's brushed."

Julia hugged the little girl and kissed her.

"Then Timmy isn't as pretty as you."

Emily giggled.

"Timmy's a boy, he's not pretty."

༄༅

One day Emily announced that Timmy would soon be having a birthday.

"He will be six." she announced proudly. "Can I get him a present please, Mummy.?"

"I expect so," agreed Paula, "Next time we go into the village. Will that be okay? When is it?"

"Twenty eighth of August." she replied at once.

"That's not for a couple of weeks, so we have plenty of time to choose something." said Paula, confident that the little girl would forget all about it by then.

༄༅

Emily was looking so healthy and rosy cheeked from spending so much time in the garden during the long hot summer, and Paula was delighted to see how well adjusted and happy her daughter looked. Because of this, she too felt happier and more relaxed and able to come to terms with her changing circumstances.

She and Julia decorated Emily's bedroom. They allowed the little girl to choose the wallpaper and furnishings, and when Julia gave her some prints of Victorian children for the wall, she was delighted, because she said that Timmy thought they were perfect.

ఐⓒ

All summer long Peter had been working in the over-grown garden. He had seen the original plans for the house, discovered in the attic by Julia and Paula, and was keen to restore a lily pond that had graced a sunken garden at the rear of the house. He had removed all the old shrubs and over-grown roses and uncovered the outer walls of the pond and had began to carefully excavate. It was hard work, but very satisfying and he was determined to have the pond fully restored before the winter set in.

Meanwhile, Julia and Paula had cleared the attic, and were systematically going through all the boxes of junk, trunks of old clothes and photographs left by the previous owner. Most stuff was disintegrating with age, but occasionally they found something in good condition.

"Do you think we will find a long lost masterpiece worth millions of pounds?" asked Paula as they sorted through a box of old newspapers and books.

"I doubt it," said Julia. "Possible, but unlikely. This house had been in the same family since it was built. It had been terribly neglected, which is why we got it at such a good price. The last owner was Alice Hartington, who was the great-granddaughter of the original owner. She was the last member of the family and almost ninety when she died. She never married, so there are no heirs. We are the first people who aren't Hartingtons to live here. A humbling thought, isn't it?"

Paula picked up a large cigar box, wiped the dust from it and opened it.

"Look at this," she said in amazement. "Hundreds of old photographs and in surprisingly good condition."

She took the box over to the table and she and Julia sat down and began to go through contents.

"Aren't these wonderful!" declared Julia. "Pure Victoriana. I love the fashions. Just look at those hats and gowns. How tiny the women's w#aists were!"

"This must be a family group," Paula said, holding up a large sepia print that portrayed two adults and three children, formally posed for the camera.

"They must be the Hartingtons, the original owners, I expect." She let out an excited little yelp. "Look, they are posed in front of the lily pond, Dad is going to be so pleased to see that."

Emily skipped into the room and went to look at the pile of pictures that was attracting her Mother and Grandmother's attention. She shuffled through them and suddenly her face lit up.

"Look Mummy," she said excitedly, waving a picture. "Here's a picture of Timmy."

Paula took the picture from her daughter's hand and saw that it was a studio portrait of a solemn little boy, with large eyes, straight blond hair and dressed in a sailor-suit.

Emily took the picture from her mother and ran to Julia.

"See, Granny," she said. "It's Timmy."

Julia adjusted her glasses and looked closely at the photograph.

"Ah, so this is what Timmy looks like, is it?"

"He don't look like him, it is him!" insisted Emily. "He always wears his sailor-suit. Can I take the picture and show him, please,"

Paula nodded and she ran from the room calling "Timmy, look what I got."

"What do you make of that?" asked Julia. "Strange, or what?"

"Very weird." agreed Paula, looking uncomfortable.

They were interrupted by Peter calling them from the garden.

"Come and see, I've at last uncovered the lily pond."

The women joined Peter outside and followed him to the sunken garden, where he showed them his handiwork. He had uncovered a large, complete, though dry, pond.

"It's in excellent condition," he said excitedly. "Considering it hasn't been touched for so long." He bent down and scraped some earth away. "See, this little wall that surrounded it is almost complete. The lion's head is the fountain, I assume. I have even found the original pots that held the marginal plants and water lilies. It really is a beauty and I intend to restore it to its former glory."

"Do you think it was deliberately filled in?" asked Julia. "It wouldn't be in such good nick if it just crumbled away, would it?"

"Maybe the Hartingtons filled it in. After all, they did have young children around, if that picture we found is anything to go by. Maybe they thought a lily pond was a danger to them."

"Don't worry, " said Peter, seeing Paula's worried face. "I don't intend filling the pond with water until I can cover it with mesh. We don't want any accidents, do we?"

Paula shuddered at the thought, but was reassured by Peter's words.

One hot day in late August Emily announced that she wanted to go into the village to get Timmy's birthday present.

"He's six tomorrow," she explained.

Paula was surprised that her daughter had accurately remembered the date.

"What would you like to buy him?" she asked.

"He wants a boat." Emily said at once. "He's a sailor boy and he likes boats."

In the village toy shop Emily took great trouble in selecting a little red plastic boat with a white sail.

"Timmy will like that," she declared, "He likes that colour."

As they left the shop there was rumbling of thunder in the distance. Paula looked up to the sky.

"We'd better hurry, sweetheart," she said taking the little girl's hand. "I think we are in for a storm. We'd better get home before it breaks."

༄༅

It was gone midnight when Paula woke. The air was hot and humid, and her night dress was sticking to her with perspiration.

A tremendous clap of thunder shook the house and lightening rent the sky, as a strong wind threw torrents of rain against the window.

Paula got up, and concerned in case the noise had woken Emily, hurried along the landing to her daughter's bedroom and opened the door.

Emily lay asleep, the red plastic boat clasped tightly in one hand. She looked peaceful and undisturbed by the fury of the storm.

Knowing that sleep was impossible for a while, Paula went down into the kitchen to make tea. She had just lit the gas under the kettle when her parents joined her.

"My word," exclaimed Julia. "It's many a year since I've seen a storm like this. It's been building up all day."

She pulled back the curtains and looked out of the window.

"Just look at that rain! It's been lashing down for hours."

"I checked on Emily," said Paula, as she poured the tea. "She was fast asleep. Amazing that this thunder didn't wake her."

Paula and her parents sat drinking their tea and watching the drama outside, as the lightening lit up the garden. Then as a rumble of thunder died away they heard the distinct sound of a child's cry.

Paula was on her feet in a second.

"Emily," she cried, as she ran upstairs to her daughter's room.

In a trice she was back.

"She's not there!" she sobbed, her face white as a sheet.

The cry came again.

"She must be outside." said Peter, running out into the garden, followed by the two women. They were heedless of the rain that drenched them.

They ran over the muddy lawn, through the shrubbery and into the sunken garden.

Peter was there first. He was horrified to see that the rain-water had poured down the sloping sides of the sunken garden and filled the newly excavated lily-pond to the brim.

A dazzling flash of lightening illuminated the pond.

"Oh my God!" he exclaimed in horror, as the terrified trio saw the tiny limp body of Emily floating face down in the water. Her pink nightdress billowed around her and her dark curls spread out from her head like sea weed.

Peter waded into the pond and scooped the child's limp body from the water, lay her on the grass and immediately began to resuscitate her, pumping water from her lungs. After what seemed like an eternity, a shudder ran through her little body and she began to breathe again.

ಸಿಧ

Later all three sat round Emily's bed as she recovered from her ordeal. Paula stroked back the damp curls from her daughter's forehead, and Julia held her hand.

The doctor was sent for and he said that Emily was a lucky little girl. Peter's quick actions had saved her life.

Seeing how upset Paula was. He went over to her and patted her hand.

"Don't go blaming yourself," he said kindly. "You weren't to know that she was going to wander off in the storm. Children often strange things. She'll be as right as nine pence in the morning, you'll see."

And she was.

ಸಿಧ

Over breakfast Paula gently questioned her daughter.

"Why did you go out in all that rain last night, darling?"

"Timmy woke me up," explained Emily. "He said it was his birthday and he wanted to sail his new boat. He said there was water in the pond now and he wanted to show me how good it sailed."

Tears welled up in her eyes.

"Mummy, he fell in." She looked distressed and tears rolled down her cheeks. "I tried to save him, but I couldn't pull him out. He was too heavy." She rubbed at her eyes. "You see, he is a big boy and six years old and I am only four. He pulled me in. He didn't mean to, but I slipped."

She looked up at Paula, her eyes big and red from crying.

"Timmy has gone now, Mummy." she said quietly. "He won't be back."

Paula shuddered as Emily added "He's in Heaven with Daddy."

Emily never mentioned Timmy again.

༄༅

Things soon got back to normal and then it was time for Emily to go to the village school. She took to it right away and everyone was pleased to see that she settled down and became a happy, normal little girl.

One day Paula and Julia started to sort through the stuff they found in the attic again. They tipped the contents of the old cigar box onto the table and found, amongst the household bills, theatre programmes and old photographs, a newspaper cutting, yellowing with age, but still quite readable.

Paula carefully unfolded it, spread it out on the table and began to read, and as she did the blood drained from her face and her hands began to shake.

The headline read.

TRAGIC DEATH OF A CHILD

Followed by this account.

Timothy Arthur Hartington of Hartington Villa, Richmond Road, drowned in the lily-pond at his home on the twenty eighth day of August 1906. It was his sixth birthday.

The inquest was told that he had been in the care of his nursemaid, Miss Amelia Jenkins, who said she was taking the boy to sail a boat, a birthday present, on the lily-pond at the rear of the house.

The child was eager to put it on the water and had run ahead of her. She followed as quickly as she could.

As she approached the sunken garden, in which the lily pond lay, she heard a splash and Timmy's voice.

"Emily, Emily, save me." he cried.

As Miss Jenkins emerged from the shrubbery she saw that the boy was lying face down in the water. She called to the gardener to help her, and he managed to pull the child from the pond. He tried to revive him, but to no avail. The boy was dead.

Miss Jenkins was asked to explain who Emily was. She said that Timmy had invented an imaginary companion, a four year old girl, whom he called by that name.

Mr.& Mrs. Hartington, who have two remaining sons, Thomas, who is four and six month old George, have ordered the lily-pond to be filled in.

ಸಿಂಡ

Paula, her face white, handed the cutting to Julia.

"When Emily fell in the pond it was the twenty eighth of August 2006," she said shakily. "Exactly a hundred years since little Timmy Hartington was drowned in the lily-pond on his sixth birthday."

WRITING EXERCISE

From time to time the Huntingdon Writers' Group has 'On The Spot Writing Exercises'. Recently we had to look at a selection of pictures, choose one, study it for ten minutes then write for twenty minutes on something triggered by the picture. The picture I chose showed a disgruntled looking bride, with a much older couple, one on either side of her. This was the story I wrote

"Please, Mummy, can't you just be nice to him for one day?"
"I was nice to him for twenty years, and where did that get me?" snapped Joan.

"Please don't spoil my day." Petra begged. "You only have to tolerate him for a few hours, and it would mean so much to me. Surely you can do that."

"Humph," Joan said sulkily. "Is that woman coming with him?"

"What woman?" Petra asked vaguely.

"Oh God!" Joan said dramatically. "He's not got yet another has he?"

"You know what Dad's like" Petra made light of the situation. "Always the charmer, so who knows."

"Oh yes," said Joan bitterly. "Always the charmer until he's married, then his wife is no longer thought worth the effort." She smiled viciously. "He even managed to charm me once."

"Well, he's my Dad and I love him. I want you both to be there on my wedding day, so please, Mummy. Do try to be nice."

"OK, darling," Joan sighed. "I'll try, but don't expect miracles."

The day of Petra and Stephen's wedding dawned bright and sunny, and all went well with the ceremony and beyond.

At the reception Joan sat stiffly next to Jim, her ex-husband, making little effort to engage in conversation, although every time there eyes met, she smiled a little too sweetly.

Joan had to admit that Jim was still a very handsome man. He was tall, with a mass of rather distinguished looking white hair. He had kept himself in good shape, she noted, glancing quickly at the way his broad shoulders filled the jacket of his morning suit.

She sipped her third glass of champagne and realised that he was getting more and more handsome with each sip. She also had to admit to herself that she was very pleased to see that he was alone. No beautiful woman accompanied him.

When Petra and Stephen left for their honeymoon, Joan realised that Jim was standing by her side as they waved them goodbye.

He gently touched her arm, looked down at her and smiled fondly.

"Didn't our daughter look beautiful." he said softly, and Joan was disturbed to find that his deep voice still gave her goose bumps. "She looked almost as lovely as her mother did on her wedding day." he continued.

Joan felt her face redden.

"A hot flush," she thought. "I am not blushing at my age!"

They walked back to the hotel bar with the rest of the guests, where Jim poured her yet another glass of champagne.

"I've missed you, Joan." he said with a gentle smile.

"Really?" she replied, looking coyly at him over the rim of her glass.

"Yes, really." he grinned. "Have you missed me?"

"Sometimes," Joan admitted. "But I don't miss the arguments, the feeling of jealousy when you chat up other women, or the lies when you stayed out late."

"Ah yes," he said. "I was a fool and you were too suspicious." he laughed softly. "But I am sure we have both mellowed. Old age does bring tolerance and contentment, don't you think?"

"Old age!" she snorted "You may be old, Jim, but I certainly am not, so let's get that straight for a start!"

"That's my girl!" he squeezed her hand. "Still as fiery as ever. Now, how about we have dinner sometime soon?"

"That would be nice." Joan said, silently thanking Petra for insisting on them both being at her wedding.

A THANK YOU LETTER
(A Writers' Group Exercise)

Dear Tom & Alice,

Thank you so much for inviting Bill and me to your dinner party last week. We really enjoyed ourselves.

The food was wonderful, although Bill says it was a little too rich for his delicate stomach. I do hope the stain comes out of the carpet OK. I always use 1001 Carpet Cleaner myself.

I love champagne, but Bill isn't used to it, and said he would have been fine had he not mixed it with all those after dinner brandies.

I told him that it was no excuse for the things he said to your mother, but he hadn't realised how over-sensitive she was. I do hope she recovered quickly from her hysterics, although she did seem very upset at the time. I was always taught that slapping a person's face was the way to cure someone in that state, although she didn't seem to appreciate it at the time. My dress ring is rather big, I know, but I trust the ice pack soon settled down the swelling. A fat lip can look so unsightly in one of mature years, don't you think?

Did I really make a pass at you, Tom? What a hoot! It would never have happened had I been sober, because I have never considered you to be in the least bit attractive, and it makes my skin crawl to think of it in the cold light of dawn. I can hardly believe that I was annoyed enough at your rebuff to spit in your face. Not very lady-like, but drink often affects me that way.

Bill would like to apologise to your niece. We both agree that she is a lovely girl, but if she goes around in that short skirt and skimpy top, what does she expect? All I can say is that it was a good job I spotted what was going on, otherwise, goodness knows what might have happened.

It's a shame about the fight though. I'm afraid I did lose control for a while. I have never been able to get used to Bill and his naughty little ways with young girls. Was that really a Ming vase? Surely not! I have seen better stuff at the Car Boot Sale.

Even so, I really shouldn't have thrown it at him. I am just sorry it missed. It would have served the so and so right had it clobbered him. Still, on the positive side, I suppose the French doors can be mended easier than a broken skull.

Tell your friend Tina that is really is a mistake to interfere in a fight between husband and wife. I know she meant well, but she really should have known better. I have sent her a get well card. It is Oak ward isn't it?

We both thought your Persian cat was adorable, and Bill wouldn't have dreamed of using her to mop up after his little accident, but to be fair to him, there was nothing else available at the time. I am sure she came up as good as new after a good shampooing.

I know that Bill shouldn't have attempted to drive after all that drink, but there's no telling him when he has had a few.

I am sure your insurance company will pay up. After all, you weren't even in the car when it was written off, were you? Those foreign cars are so flimsy. No wonder so much damage was inflicted by our scruffy little family saloon! To be honest, whoever heard of a Maserati anyway?

Needless to say we had a great time and enjoyed meeting all your friends, though I must say that some of them weren't exactly friendly. Maybe they are just shy! We did try to break the ice, but they just didn't respond, even though some of Bill's practical jokes were hilarious!

Must dash. See you soon, I hope. We can't wait for your next do.

Best wishes and get well soon.

Love from

Gloria and Bill

My Cousin Alex
(Written by Molly Holohan-Green in 2005 aged 9)

He's as bouncy as a trampoline in the back yard,
As cute as a pop-star at the premier,
He's a bright and breezy afternoon,
He is the beautiful scent of roses being swept through by the breeze.
He is as sweet as a strawberry with cream.
He is my cousin Alexander

HAPPY
EVER AFTER
(A 21st Century Fairy Tale)

"Hello, Chris. Where's everybody?"

Chris looked up from digging the garden to see his Godfather walking down the path towards him.

"Hi, Uncle Julian," he said wearily. "I'm afraid I am the only one here today. Dad and the boys have gone to see the Rovers play in the cup tie and Mum has gone shopping."

"I would have thought that you would have gone to the match as well. I know how much you love your football."

Chris straightened his back.

"I do, but I can't afford it." He said glumly. "I still haven't found a job, I haven't got any money and I still owe Mum and Dad twenty quid, so I said I would work off the debt doing a few jobs around the house and garden."

"What would you say if I told you that you could go to the match?" said Uncle Julian with a twinkle in his eye.

"Impossible," said Chris grimly. "It's a nice idea, but I haven't got a ticket."

"Oh yes you have!" said his Godfather triumphantly. "At least, I have. A good friend of mine gave it to me, but ..." he smiled archly, smoothing back his lavender coloured hair. " ...it's hardly my kind of thing. I simply hate football. It's such a rough game, although I have to say that all those strapping young men in their shorts do look very attractive."

He smiled dreamily, then, snapping back to reality, he added. "You are welcome to the ticket, my boy."

Chris's face lit up, but the smile died on his lips at once.

"It's really nice of you, Uncle, but it is absolutely impossible." he sighed deeply. "It's freezing cold, I don't have a warm coat, or money for the bus to the stadium."

"No problem, lovely," beamed his Godfather. "Take my car. My sheepskin coat is on the back seat, wear that and welcome!" He waved his hand airily, dismissing his nephew's words of gratitude. "Away with you and enjoy yourself. I'll wait here for your return."

Chris grinned broadly at his uncle.

"If you are really sure … "he said excitedly.

"Go on!" Uncle Julian said, smiling broadly.

Chris ran upstairs and grabbed the woolly Rovers hat that he had been wearing to matches since his schooldays, and dashed back downstairs to get the car keys from Uncle Julian.

"There's just one thing, sweetie." said his Godfather looking serious. "You must be home by six o clock. I have a date with a rather special friend at seven, and I really cannot be late." He looked coyly at his Godson. "You won't let me down, Chris, will you?"

"I promise I will be home in good time." Chris reassured him. "Thank you so much, Uncle, you are an angel."

"One does one's best, my boy. Now off you go or you will miss the bully-off, or whatever they call it."

Chris got to the stadium just before the three o clock kick-off, raced up the terrace steps and found the seat number indicated on his ticket. It was right on the aisle and he couldn't help noticing that he was sitting next to a pretty young blonde girl wearing a Rovers scarf and rosette. She smiled as he took his seat, showing perfect white teeth and the cutest dimples he had ever seen. He had never seen such a lovely girl in all his life. He didn't have time to say anything to her, because the referee blew his whistle and play started.

The game was really exciting, and Chris and the girl jumped and cheered as they followed the end to end play. When Rovers almost scored they looked at each other and let out cries of disappointment. Once the Rovers striker actually put the ball in the net, but when the referee judged it to be off-side, the girl jumped to her feet, stumbled, and almost fell into Chris's lap, as she berated the referee. She managed to regain her balance, then looking extremely embarrassed; she smiled and offered Chris a peppermint sweet. He accepted and as he sucked his precious gift, he wished she had actually fallen into his lap; the idea was very attractive indeed.

Then along came disaster. Just before half time United scored.

The girl was distraught, so Chris tried to console her.

"Don't worry," he said with a confidence he didn't really feel. "They'll come back in the second half. There's plenty of time for them to score, you'll see."

"I hope you're right." she said with a wan smile.

At half time the girl shared her flask of coffee with him, as they discussed the Rovers, their prospects, favourite players and performances.

By the end of the interval, Chris was madly in love. She was the perfect girl in his eyes. Not only was she beautiful, intelligent, and had a sweet personality, she was a knowledgeable football fan!

The second half was equally as exciting as the first, and just before close of play Rovers equalised.

Both Chris and the girl were beside themselves with excitement and leapt from their seats with joy, hugging each other in ecstasy. Then they both looked embarrassed and sat down again.

There were no more goals in the first half of extra time, and Chris and his new friend chatted nervously in the short interval, desperately hoping United wouldn't score again.

She was shaking and breathless.

"I can't stand this tension!! She breathed. "I'm so glad you are here. It helps to have someone to share it with. I'm Charmian Prince. What's your name?"

His reply was drowned in the roar of the crowd as the teams resumed playing.

Their joy was unconfined when Rovers scored in the dying minutes of the game to win 2-1, thus assuring their place in the Final.

Charmian hugged Chris again, and much to his delight planted a kiss on his cheek with such enthusiasm that she knocked off his woolly hat, but he didn't notice, all he was aware of was Charmian's rosy cheeks, sparkling eyes and dimples. He really was hopelessly in love.

Suddenly he spotted the clock above the stadium. It was five forty five. He had exactly fifteen minutes to get the car back to Uncle Julian. He couldn't let him down after all his kindness to him. He had no time to explain to Charmian. So squeezing her hand, he kissed her cheek briefly and ran down the terrace steps to the car park, leaving his woolly hat on the ground at her feet. She waved sadly at his departing figure, then spotting the hat, she picked it up and smiled.

It was a love sick Chris who had to spend the next day catching up on his chores and studying for his exams.

He was determined to get a job in computers and knew that keeping up with his course work was the only way to succeed, but he couldn't get the lovely Charmian out of his mind. He longed to see her again and pinned his hopes on seeing her at the next Rover's home game. Mind you, it would be like looking for a needle in a hay stack.

Meanwhile, Charmian was having more luck. She was just as keen to see Chris again and had spotted the name 'C. Cindrellis' and an address on the label inside his woolly cap, so after work on Monday she drove over to the house, hoping he was still living there. She wanted to return his precious hat to him in person.

When she knocked at the door, his mother let her in.

"I found this after the Rover's game on Saturday and wondered if it belonged to anyone here."

Seeing such a beautiful girl, both of Chris's brothers, Charles and Colin lay claim to it, and although she knew it didn't belong to either of them, she let them try it on. It fell over Charles's ears and it sat like a pimple on top of Colin's big head.

"I knew it wasn't either of you," she said showing her dimples. "My Mr. Cindrellis was far better looking than either of you." adding "Sorry, no offence." when she saw their disappointment.

"Call Chris down." said their father. "Let him try it on."

"How can it be his?" the brothers sneered. "He couldn't afford a ticket, so he wasn't even there."

"Oh yes he was." said Uncle Julian, who had just arrived with his new special friend. "I gave him a ticket."

Charmian gave him her sweetest smile.

"That was nice of you," she said,

"I'll call him down." Said Chris's mother. "He's studying in his room."

As soon as Charmian saw Chris her face broke into a radiant smile, and she handed him the hat. He put it on, it fitted perfectly of course. He grinned happily at the assembled company, and then turned back to Charmian.

"Hello," he said. "I am so happy to see you again. I've thought of nothing else since we met."

"Oh how romantic!" declared Uncle Julian, clasping the arm of his friend. "They make such a lovely couple, don't you think?"

Chris and Charmian spent the rest of the evening together and discovered that they had much more in common than their favourite football team.

Chris showed her the complicated advanced computer course he was taking, and explained that although he was highly qualified, he was still finding it difficult to find a job, after being made redundant from his last post.

"I may be able to help," she smiled. "You may have heard of my father. He is known as William Prince the Computer King. He is looking for a bright young man to groom to be his successor when he retires from Prince Computers in a few years time. Would you like me to arrange an appointment with him?"

"That would be fantastic" beamed Chris. "You are wonderful, Charmian. It's no wonder I fell in love with you at first sight!"

Charmian blushed prettily "I feel the same about you." she said softly, giving him a gentle kiss on the cheek.

The following Wednesday Chris went to see Charmian's father at Prince Computers. After the interview Mr. Prince offered Chris a job at once, having been impressed by the young man's knowledge and pleasant personality.

"My daughter seems to have taken a great shine to you, young man." he said. "I can deny that girl nothing. Now if you promise me that you will take good care of her, you can start work here on Monday." He then mentioned a salary that took Chris's breath away.

As he was leaving, Mr. Prince called him back.

"My daughter told me where you met. It just so happens that I am a director of Rovers, as she may have already told you. Anyway, here's a season ticket, which allows you onto the terraces or into the director's box, if you prefer." He smiled. "I know Charmian prefers the terraces, so you will be doing me a favour by looking after her. I have always worried about her being on her own. Now I know she will be in good hands."

"Thank you, sir." Chris beamed. "I won't let you down, I promise."

It was an ecstatic Chris who escorted the lovely Charmian on the coach to the away match the next Saturday. He couldn't believe his luck. Was it really only last Saturday that he had been stuck at home gardening, with no money, no job, no prospects and no girlfriend? Now he had it all thanks to his Godfather Uncle Julian.

Chris slipped his arm round Charmian, kissed her cheek and sighed happily.

"We're bound to live happily ever after." he whispered.

"Of course." she agreed.

ANGELS
(Written By Molly Holohan-Green in 2005 aged 9)

In the middle of it all,
Comes angels ... hoorah!
In the middle of it all,
Come the devils ... aahh!